ALASKAN GOLD
Non Illegitimus Carborundum
By
Rosalyn Stowell

Copyright 2012
Publisher: R. E. Stowell
Fairbanks, Alaska

Cover photo by Virginia Maxine Stevens
Photo of the author by Samantha Stowell

Other books by Rosalyn Stowell
Don't Use A Chainsaw In The Kitchen (Cookbook)
The Beginning - Book 1
The Dark Of Night - Book 2
The Dawn - Book 3
Alaskan Alibi

Chapter 1

Just what was she doing here? Whatever made her decide to come North to see her inheritance for herself? Did she take everyone's advice? NoOoo, she did it her way. When would she ever learn, sometimes it pays to look before leaping. This time she really outdid herself.

"But Dad, you know Grampa would have wanted me to go up and take care of this myself. I just wish I would have gone while he was still alive. But Bill was set against it and you and Mom sided with him. You know I need some time away, now that our engagement is broken."

"Honey, that's just a lover's spat. Bill will be over tonight to patch things up. Then you can forget about this trip, just accept the offer that's been made for the property and get on with marrying Bill and starting a family."

Was that only yesterday? Her family was certainly against her coming up here. Bill had not come over and here she was, in the middle of nowhere. Maybe they were right, but it was a little late to think of that now.

When the letter arrived from her Grandfather's attorney, informing her of his death and that she was the sole Beneficiary of his Estate, she had mourned the loss of the gruff old man. She had not seen him very often, but there was always a special bond between them. His letters were brief, usually once a year events. She sent numerous little notes to him through the years and so their affection for each other grew.

Her Grandfather went to Alaska after the death of his wife 35 years ago and found the solitary life of a miner led to the peace of mind he longed for.

But none of that told her what she was doing here, There must be at least a zillion mosquitoes trying to carry her back to their nest or did mosquitoes nest? Having lived all her life in high desert country, she was never bothered much by bugs. Scorpions and snakes, yes, bugs, no. She couldn't remember ever being more uncomfortable in her life. Somehow the outfit that was so nice to travel in just didn't seem appropriate for the present situation.

This was a whole different world from the one she left the night before. The plane flight to Fairbanks, uneventful, the airport, nothing extraordinary. Certainly nothing led her to believe that she should possibly sit down and rethink her idea of carrying on the old man's work. The young man that flew her to this remote airfield seemed a bit surprised that no one was here to pick her up but evidently was used to rather eccentric behavior. The 2 seater plane certainly made too much noise to carry on conversation. Her bag was easy to hand out, he didn't even step out of the plane or shut it off, just waved and left.

She was surprised at the admiring glances from some of the men at the Fairbanks airport. She knew she was no beauty and a bit too well developed for current fashions. She was in good condition from working on her parents' ranch, but most men didn't seem to appreciate a woman that could buck bales of hay, throw a calf, doctor or brand it and she just couldn't catch the knack of looking helpless. But now, when she was really feeling helpless, where was the handsome fellow that was supposed to rush to her rescue? He was certainly taking his own sweet time about it.

Well, rather than let the mosquitoes pack her off and it would probably be in the wrong direction at that, she might as well start walking. She knew pretty much the direction to go from references in letters and some old photos. Of course they were all in the bottom of her duffle bag. She was very glad she hadn't given in and bought the nice luggage. After a few steps in fashionable shoes, she decided that if there were no one to give her a ride, there would also be no one to see her change her clothes. Having grabbed the first things she could find, she quickly stripped and was soon dressed in jeans, sweatshirt and athletic shoes. She picked up her bags and started walking in what she hoped was the right direction.

A mile or so later, she was not so sure. Grampa was rather vague about distances, but she was sure he said his cabin was only a mile from that cleared area called an airstrip. Now she wished she had picked out a T-shirt instead of the aptly named sweatshirt. Wasn't it supposed to be cold in Alaska? It must be at least 90 degrees but at least the mosquitoes had thinned out a bit. There were only a million or so in her escort, now.

The trees were a surprise, with their lovely green leaves and white bark. The birch and a few aspen made an arch over most of the road so at least she was in the shade most of the time. The thick inviting cushion of moss under the trees only tempted her once to sit and relax. She was immediately swarmed by some tiny black flies with white feet that made the mosquitoes seem almost welcome in contrast.

There were a few spruce and an occasional tamarack tree through the birch and aspen. Ever so often, there were low rounded hillocks on the gentle slope of the hill she was gradually climbing. The moss and trees grew in an unbroken carpet over them so they must be natural.

The varieties of wildflowers were a surprise to her as only a few flowers managed to grow in the high desert in Oregon. Here, there were flowers everywhere, in the moss and along the road. The air was filled with their lovely perfume. She was so enchanted, she almost forgot how tired and sticky she felt, when rounding a corner, she saw Grampa's cabin. Of course it was her cabin now, but that was only on paper. It would always be Grampa's cabin.

Grampa patented the claims soon after discovering them, so the land and cabin were really hers. She had heard of cabins being burned on unpatented claims, because the regulations had changed since they were built.

The cabin seemed to be part of the land it sat upon. It was low to the ground, made of logs with a sod roof. Flowers were blooming profusely on the roof and along the front of the cabin. There was a nice little creek running about a hundred yards down the hill from the cabin and the sound of running water made her realize how thirsty and hot she really was. Grampa sent her a key, several years ago, when he first invited her to come up. She had it on a chain in her purse so didn't have to worry about getting in.

The inside of the cabin was a pleasant surprise. It was small, about 18 by 24 feet, but everything was built into it's own niche to make a very efficient and homey appearance. It was cool and dark, almost like a cave, after her walk, but as soon as she raised the shades and sunlight poured in, she had a feeling of being home. Thank goodness there was a screen door besides the hand-hewn door, so the mosquitoes couldn't feed on her indefinitely. What did the people use to keep them at bay? She would have to ask the first person she saw.

The walls were smooth logs, the ceiling was of small peeled poles. Across the center of the cabin was a support log with book shelves built from the ceiling to the back of the old couch that worked as a room divider. A table was between the couch and the front of the cabin, with chairs pulled up around it. The other side of the front of the cabin was the cooking area, with a propane stove, cabinets and countertop. There was a sink but no water flowed from the tap. She would have to see about that.

Beyond the couch was the sleeping area with a double bed and a dresser. A barrel made into a heating stove sat in the fourth corner with a door between it and the bed. When she opened the door, she was surprised to find a small shed attached to the cabin. Evidently it was for storage and seemed to be well filled. She would have to go through all of Grampa's belongings and she hated the thought. It could wait until tomorrow. Right now, she needed something to eat and drink, then a good long sleep. Why hadn't she considered the possibility of no available food? She, who everyone considered so level headed? Nothing she had done in the last week seemed in character. It just had been such a shock to get the news about Grampa. He was not ill, she received a letter from him about a month ago. He seemed his usual self, going on about the business of getting ready for the brief summer's mining season.

He described his set-up and all the preparations necessary for mining. He mildly complained about all the permits needed to mine on his own property. He seemed to relegate them to the status of mosquitoes, just part of living and working in the beautiful Northland. He did mention some of his neighbors by name over the years so she was quite sure she would be able to practically recognize them on sight. He also mentioned some of the government agents that he dealt with from year to year. His letter was the usual chatty letter, filled with information that always made her feel such a part of his life. She felt as though she would recognize every part of these claims as she walked over them tomorrow.

As she looked around the cabin, she discovered water in a cooler on the countertop and a can of spaghetti that she ate without benefit of heating it up first. She was so tired, she decided to take a nap and clean up the layer of dust later.

She awoke with a start, some time later, feeling disoriented and chilled. There was a sound outside that did not seem right. Cautiously, she peeked out the window and jumped back with a little shriek. Not 6 inches from her nose had been another nose, black and furry. As she went back to the window, she saw a large black furry rump disappearing into the trees on the other side of the road. A bear. She didn't have any idea there might be bears around the cabin and the inside door was still open. There was only the screen door between her and a rather large potentially dangerous animal. She certainly didn't feel tired now.

When she checked her watch, it read 5:30 which wasn't much help. She didn't know how long she slept and whether it was morning or evening. Looking at the sun didn't help, either. It didn't set until August and this was only June. She realized while walking to the cabin that the sun never seemed to be directly overhead. It just seemed to circle around the sky. That would take some getting used to. She finally noticed the shotgun hanging over the door. She checked it out and found it was a 12 gauge with a box of slugs, suitable for large animals and a box of shot for grouse or ptarmigan. After seeing the bear, she decided to start carrying it while checking the outdoor facilities.

Sure enough, there was a small outhouse a suitable downwind distance from the cabin. On her way back to the cabin, she noticed a fenced patch of green and found a badly overgrown garden. If she wasn't deluding herself, there appeared to be some lettuce and other recognizable leaves showing through the weeds. That would definitely be a priority job, right after cleaning the cabin.

As she started cleaning the cabin, she found little notes written by her grandfather. Some were yellow with age but all were written to her. It was almost like visiting with him and made the cabin seem even more like home. The notes were about how different things worked around the cabin, how to operate his old dozer and where it should be parked, where his old 4 wheel drive pickup should be and some of it's quirks. She found some little bottles of bug repellant and put one in her pocket. She also found some little green coils to burn, for ridding larger areas of mosquitoes, then a can of Buhach and instructions on how to use it. It could be burned to rid the cabin of almost all bugs or sprinkled to keep ants away.

As she dusted and became acquainted with her new home, she discovered a complete stock of groceries, the small notes giving her the approximate amounts needed to stay over the winter. She was not sure whether or not she even wanted to consider the possibility, but the more she thought about it, the better she liked the idea. But first there was this summer to get through. She needed to find out if she could make a living here or not. Her grandfather did some trapping in the winter and the traps still hung out in the shed. She didn't know if he did it from necessity or to keep boredom at bay. But she would have to consider that this was a remote area. There would be no close winter neighbors to visit with, no doctor to go to and no corner grocery to pick up something she needed or wanted.

After her cleaning and unpacking was under control, she decided to start on the garden. Grampa had evidently just gotten it planted shortly before his death. The weeds were doing extremely well, she would have to proceed with caution. She soon found that the rows were planted in raised beds so was able to proceed at a faster pace. First, she cleared the center walkways and was amazed at the difference this made. Standing back and looking over the progress made, she decided to take a walk up the little canyon and look around a bit and give her back a break.

Carrying the shotgun gave her a sense of security as she hiked up the trail toward the "workings" and she enjoyed the warm fresh air. She found the old sluice box, dam and pipe right where Grampa's notes said they would be. Of course, what did she expect? Them to have moved since he wrote? Grampa had been preparing for her arrival for the last 5 years or so, going by the notes.

The water looked so inviting, she decided to take a swim to clear away the sweat, dust and grime of the day. She would have to figure out Grampa's water system later. She stripped off her clothing and dove into the water and thought her breathing and heart had stopped. It was COLD. How could water that looked so inviting be so bone chilling cold? As she surfaced, she was aware of a shadow on the water where there shouldn't have been a shadow and immediately thought of the bear. Bears could swim. The gun was over on her pile of clothes. Well, holding her eyes shut wasn't going to make it go away so she might as well open them.

As she blinked the water from her eyes, she was looking into a pair of the most beautiful blue eyes she had ever seen in her life. She was almost afraid to look any farther, the rest of him could not possibly live up to those eyes. Ah, but the rest of him could and did. What a gorgeous man. She couldn't remember anyone of this description in any of Grampa's notes or letters. Of course, Grampa wouldn't be interested in the way his eyes were the blue of a summer sky or hair like the sun shining on a field of golden grain.

For his part, he was so surprised to discover the person in the pond was a girl and a rather well built girl at that, that he hadn't noticed the close scrutiny he was getting. She was tall and not a slender girl. But she didn't have any excess fat on her frame, either. Some people would consider her too heavy, unless they were to see her as he was, now. She looked like a well trained athlete. Her hair had come loose from the braid she traveled in and hung down the middle of her back and front and covered some of her more interesting parts from his gaze.

She had just remembered where her clothes were and that her hair was the only thing between her and total nudity. She didn't know who this fellow could be, but just because he looked like one of her better dreams didn't mean he might not be dangerous. Especially in her present state of dress. She casually turned from him and started wading deeper into the pond. It took all her willpower not to rush to her clothes and the gun. But she was determined to act as though this were not in the least unusual. Also, she was determined not to let him know she was freezing to death in this liquid ice. It was summer, the sun was hot. Why wasn't the still pond at least slightly warm?

Keeping the shiver from her voice, she called back to him, "Come on in, the water's fine."

If he came in, she could get to her cloths before he could get his breath.

Without even stopping to think, he peeled off his

shirt, boots and socks and dove in, just as she hoped he would. She had been edging her way to her clothes and as soon as he started his dive, she scrambled up the bank, scooped up her clothes and shotgun and ran for the brush. As she frantically pulled on her clothes, she heard him come to the surface with a shout of pure shock and surprise. "This water's freezing and where the devil did you go?"

Deciding now was not a good time to introduce herself, she sat down and held very still. She could see him sputtering and cursing his way to the bank and climbing up to his clothes. He was swinging his arms and trying to work circulation back. "M'god that water's cold. How did she stand it and where did she disappear to? I know I've been out here too long, I'm starting to hallucinate dream girls in ponds of water where no sane person would possibly be."

He looked around and not seeing anyone, peeled off his wet jeans and wrung them out. Still she did not move, knowing that if she did, he would spot her immediately. He pulled the damp jeans back on and finished dressing. Looking around one last time, he started hiking up the trail on the other side of the little valley. She could hear him muttering about his own sanity as he went and was inclined to worry about her own, also.

After he has been out of sight for several minutes, she got up and went back down toward the cabin. The dozer is not where it is supposed to be, maybe Grampa had moved it and not had a chance to put it back. She would have to look around some more. At least a dozer left tracks on the ground that she could follow and see which direction it had gone.

Later, at the cabin, she relaxed as she combed the tangles out of her hair. She supposed she should cut it, it would be much easier to take care of in some ways, but long, it was always easy to just twist up and pin to go out. It was her main claim to beauty in an age where most women cut their hair in cute, short styles. But she was not a cute sort of person and knew it would not suit her. She still had no idea of whether it was night or day, but was very tired, so decided to nap a while. This time she would at least close the door. There was a radio near the bed and she was pleasantly surprised to find the batteries were still in good condition. She was more surprised to hear that it was almost midnight. Considering this, she prepared for bed. There were nails and pegs set into the logs to use for hanging anything that was wanted close to hand. There was no regular closet, so she folded Grampa's clothes carefully and hung all her clothes on the pegs near the bed. Thank goodness she could use the same wardrobe in the summer here, that she used on the ranch. But she could see that she would need some waterproof boots and would need to pick up some perishable goods, like eggs, cheese and bread. Although since Grampa had a lot of flour on hand, she could bake tomorrow. The smell of fresh bread baking should bring any possible neighbors to investigate. With thoughts of the blue eyed stranger munching on a cinnamon roll on her mind, she fell asleep.

Chapter 2

When she arose the next morning, she ate a quick breakfast, started a batch of bread dough rising and went out to work in the garden. There was an old tiller behind the shed that she got started and the rest of the row walkways were cleared by the time the bread dough was ready to punch down and shape. As she was walking toward the cabin, she noticed the rain gutters all emptied into a large tank under the eaves of the cabin. The valve was turned off, leading into the cabin and was the reason she had no water at the sink. Of course this setup only worked in the summer and water had to be hauled in the winter. This rain water would not be very good drinking water, the spring had much better water for that, but it would give her water for washing up, cleaning and cooking. There was also an ingenious shower arrangement beside the tank, that relied on a warm sunny day to heat the water. But it was bound to be warmer than her brief swim, yesterday.

She shaped the dough into 2 loaves of bread and made the cinnamon rolls she had been thinking about out of the remaining dough. She would have to get her grandfather's sourdough pot going again if she was going to do this often. As she was waiting for the dough to raise enough to bake, she looked through the title of some of the books on the bookshelves. While she was dusting yesterday or was it the day before, she didn't take time to give more than a cursory glance. There was a good selection of reading materials, ranging from novels to the classis to how-to-do-it books from the State Cooperative Extension Service. She could get a complete education on almost anything right here from these bookshelves. She had stuck a few of her own favorite books in her duffle bag, so she added them to the already overflowing bookshelves. It was like seeing some old friends among faces that would become new friends and gave her a warm feeling of really belonging.

As the rolls were cooking and the bread was cooling, she prepared a quick lunch and was not even surprised when she heard the knock on her door. It seemed like an extension of the fantasy she had woven about the blue eyed stranger and only fitting that he show up now. However, when she opened the door, she was startled to find it was not "her" stranger but someone else's. This man was only a bit taller than she was and was dark haired with brown eyes. He looked equally surprised to see her.

"I'm looking for Joe Akins. Can you tell me where I can find him?"

Now it was her turn for surprise, "I'm Jo Akins, well, actually JoAnna Akins, may I help you?"

He stepped back and looked at her more closely.

"This must be some mistake. I have a letter from the main office stating that a Joe Akins was going to be working this ground now that Jeremy Akins has passed away. I am supposed to come out and check the operation to assure that the environmental standards are being met. Even though these are patented claims, there are still standards that must be met. I would appreciate having Joe Akins drop by the office in Fairbanks at the earliest possible time."

She could see him sereptiously smelling the delicious odor of the baking cinnamon rolls, but they were for her fantasy, not some self important fellow that didn't believe she was the person he was looking for. He was rather good looking, but really took himself very seriously. Grampa had told her quite a lot about some of these fellows. Most of them were well meaning, but a bit misguided, in his estimation. This one looked about 25 years old, only a year or two older than she was. He didn't seem to even notice she was female. He seemed to think she had "Joe" stashed somewhere back in the cabin and was deliberately concealing him from being questioned.

As it became apparent that she was not going to invite him in and give him one of those tantalizing cinnamon rolls, he stiffly walked back to his truck and drove off. She giggled a bit as she realized he had taken the dead end road that ended in a swamp just out of sight of the cabin. The correct term was tundra, but to her it was still a swamp.

There was evidence of traffic across it during

extremely dry or frozen weather. If he wasn't careful, he would be good and stuck in short order. She removed the rolls from the oven and liberally buttered the tops with some of the canned butter she found on the shelves. They were delicious. She really should have offered one to the man. But he managed to ruffle her the wrong way with his attitude. She didn't understand it, she was usually very easy going and slow to anger. Of course this whole adventure was out of character for her. Her small circle of friends thought she was coming north to make a fortune as a gold miner. Her ex-fiance had expected her to accept the offer to buy the property that accompanied the letter from Grampa's attorney. He already had planned how to spend the money on improvements to his small ranch and was livid when she refused. He would not accept her explanation that she at least wanted to see the land her Grampa loved so much. Now she wished she hadn't given in to her fiancé's demand that she stay there instead of accepting Grampa's request that she come visit last summer.

Bill had been adamant and accused her of not ever thinking of anyone but herself, that if she wouldn't think of him, at least stay and help out her family. She was shaken out of her reverie by a loud pounding on her door. When she opened it, she was not surprised to see her visitor of a few minutes ago standing there, red of face.

"Ummmm, I seem to be stuck. Could you possibly help me out?" he asked.

She guessed now would be as good a time as any to check out the old 4-wheel drive pick-up that was in the storage building near the garden. She had no idea whether it would start or if there was even any gas in it. The keys were on a peg by the door, so she pocketed them while trying to remember Grampa's note on the quirks of the old truck. This should be interesting, she thought, as she swung the heavy door open. Luckily, she remembered about the trick catch on the door so it looked like she knew what she was doing. She remembered the on-off fuel switch hidden under the seat and tried the starter. To her amazement, it started immediately, so she pulled out into the yard. Maybe it would be best to make sure there was a chain or tow rope in the back before she played rescuer to this fellow. He looked like he couldn't believe she could do it and not above giving her a bad time trying to be self sufficient and female, too. It was a good thing she was raised on a working cattle ranch and was used to doing anything that was required so was used to physical hard work.

After finding a good hefty chain in the back of the truck, she bowed elaborately, "Lead on,, McDuff."

When they arrived at his truck, she could see that he had tried to get unstuck by continuing to rev the engine and rock the truck back and forth until it now sat with mud clear up onto the doors and he had climbed out a window to get out and go for help. She wasn't sure that the old truck had enough power to pull it out. There was a shovel in the back of the truck which she put in the back corner pocket on the old truck, after letting him use it to dig out a spring shackle under his truck. The chain was wrapped around the shovel handle then down to the spring shackle of the stuck truck. He looked at her in surprise, "Will that really work?"

"Well, if you get back in yours and give as much help as possible, maybe this will supply enough lift to get you out."

She checked to make sure the old truck was in 4-wheel drive and as soon as he started his truck, she eased forward to tighten the chain slowly, then kept easing forward, slowly lifting and pulling his truck up and out of the hole. She couldn't believe how smoothly it went and evidently, neither could he. The look on his face made her wish for her camera. She calmly unhitched the chain, put the shovel back in the bed of the truck and drove off as though this were an every day event. She wasn't about to admit she was as surprised as he, that it worked so smoothly.

He hurriedly turned his truck around and followed her back to the cabin. She had already parked the truck and was walking back to the cabin when he pulled up. He jumped out and came over to her. "I want to thank you for helping me and I'm sorry if I sounded doubting of who you are, earlier. Could I start over and do this properly? My name is Will Turner and I work for the Environmental Conservation Society. We are supposed to check each working mine, once a month, to test for water quality. We are supposed to make sure that most of the Miners are reclaiming their worked ground to make this beautiful virgin wilderness able to support a new forest and animal life. I don't think they will ever be able to do that, this ecosystem is too fragile to be ruined and then reclaimed. They are ruining the fisheries also. You do not have to do the reclamation work, since these are patented claims, but you do have to follow the other regulations."

"What happens to the Miners that you find not living up to the regulations?"

"I turn the papers in at our office and they take steps to insure that the proper State of Federal agencies do their jobs. They tend to let some of these violators slide on through, without prosecuting them. My job is to find these violators and if the proper Agency doesn't do it's job, we bring suit against them and the violator."

"Why do you want to bring suit against them?"

"When I came up here, earlier this year, I found that a lot of the Miners are not following the regulations. In fact, I think it would be safe to say that none of them are. This State is so beautiful and still unspoiled by man, that I just have to do my part to keep it in it's pristine condition."

Somehow she just couldn't start an argument with him, without knowing more of the facts. But it seemed that an industry that had been in existence over a hundred years with absolutely no regulation, should have already made a desolate wasteland of the entire State if what he said was true. So he was a newcomer to the State and only had her own residency beat by a few months. Well, she would start research of her own to see how accurate his facts were. In the meantime she supposed it would be the neighborly thing to do, to invite him in for a cup of coffee and a cinnamon roll. He was trying to be nice.

"Would you care for coffee? It's only instant but it's hot."

"I would love some, most of the people out here are not too friendly."

"I can't say that I blame them, you are trying to put them out of business, aren't you?"

"No, if they follow the regulations, I can't do anything to stop them ruining the land."

"Did you ever consider that your attitude might have something to do with theirs?"

"What's wrong with my attitude, I'm only stating the truth?"

"As you see it, maybe you are. But there are usually two sides to every story and it doesn't sound like you have ever listened to any of theirs. Have you tried being polite? Sometimes it works wonders." By now she wasn't so sure she wanted to give him instant coffee, even, at least not in a cup.

"Polite? I'm always polite. Miners are just a bunch of pig-headed ruffians, intent on doing things their way or not at all."

"Well, thanks. As a pig-headed ruffian, I withdraw the offer of coffee and would like you to remove yourself from the premises. I would rather be a pig-headed ruffian than a chauvinistic encephalitic simian."

So saying, she stomped her way into the cabin, leaving stunned silence behind her. So much for not starting an argument with him.

He started to follow her, thought better of it, walked back to his truck and left.

She stepped back outside and was watching his dust cloud disappear around the bend when she heard a chuckle behind her. Whirling around, she saw an old man, small of stature, with snow white hair. The wide grin on his face was infectious and she grinned back and they both started laughing.

"By the way, young lady, just what is a chauvinistic encephalitic simian?"

"I think it's a fanatical ape with water on the brain or something like that. I read the expression once in a book and always longed for the chance to use it. I'm just amazed that I remembered it now."

"You certainly did give that feller a setdown. You should have red hair. By the way, my name is Harlan Henry and I have some claims over on the next creek. Guess I'm your closest neighbor, in that direction. That's also the way the wind was blowing earlier and unless my nose was playing tricks on me, you were baking?"

"Yes, I was. Would you care for a cup of coffee and a cinnamon roll?" Somehow it seemed like she already knew Harlan Henry. Grampa had written and talked about him a lot. They had been great friends and she would like to be friends with him, too.

"My name is Jo Akins, Grampa told me a lot about you and some of the times you two got into scrapes together. Come on in."

As she heated the water, they talked about the garden and what types of things she could count on growing here in the Alaskan Interior. She was surprised by the variety of things she could grow easily and some of the things that were marginal, depending on the weather. As she listened, she thought that a greenhouse would be a priority item on her list of things she would like to add to the yard. Most of the vegetables she grew back at the ranch would grow here, with the exception of a sure crop of corn. Almost none of the fruits would grow, but there were a lot of wild berries to help make up for that. Mr. Henry was a treasure house of knowledge on living in the "Bush" and she was a more than eager student.

As he was leaving, he paused at the door and seemed to think over what he was about to say. Finally he spoke, "Your dozer is over at Cleve Morse's place. He had no right to borrow it and shouldn't give you any guff about bringing it back. But he is not always predictable, if you like, I can go see him about returning it."

"I thank you for letting me know where it is, but I have to learn to stand on my own. If I have any trouble, I'll appreciate your help but for now, I'll go see him in the morning."

He nodded his head, "I thought that would be

your answer. You're a lot like Jeremy and I think you will do just fine. Thanks for the cinnamon rolls, it's been ages since I had any that good. Come on over, I'll look forward to visiting with you, any time."

Chapter 3

The next morning was bright and sunny, so she decided to walk over to find her dozer. She weeded for a couple of hours, earlier, and was making quite a bit of progress in the garden. She could start harvesting the leaf lettuce immediately and was looking forward to having some for dinner.

As she walked, with the shotgun casually under her arm, she thought of her final argument with Bill. She had drifted into being "sort of" engaged to him because it was expected of her. His property adjoined her father's and would be a nice place once it had some time and money spent on it. If she were honest with herself, she didn't love Bill and doubted that he had ever loved her. He loved the idea of her family helping set his ranch up. He was good looking and knew it. He made no secret of his other girlfriends but she was supposed to stay quietly at home and wait for his attentions.

Everyone told her how lucky she was to have such a handsome fellow wanting her, since she was no beauty. Now, since their last row, when he told her all he wanted was what she could help him accomplish, she knew she was lucky not to have married him. Her parents tried to convince her that he was only speaking from hurt feelings, but she knew in her heart that he was telling the truth. How could she ever have considered marriage to him? She would be better off staying here and never marrying anyone. She could become a female hermit. Maybe she had fancied herself in love with him or maybe even been a bit in love, why else would she have this sad, sorry feeling? It was probably just hurt feelings. No one liked feeling like a fool and that is what she felt like, a fool. Only a fool would have ever considered marrying him to start with. Now that she had that settled, she started paying attention to her surroundings. From the hand drawn map of the area with all the local miners marked in that Grampa had on the wall of the cabin, she realized she was almost at Cleve Morse's workings.

As she neared the worked area, she could see that Grampa's dozer was being used to push the material up for a loader to feed into the large sluice box arrangement. A man saw her standing there and came over. He was a tall, heavy-set middle aged man that once had been a fine looking man. But he looked like a beer bottle, like the one in his hand, had become his best friend. He was glaring at her and as he neared enough to be heard over the sound of the equipment he started yelling. "Get off my land and go do your snooping somewhere else."

She started to explain about the dozer, when he waved her words aside and told her he owned it now. He said he had purchased the dozer from

Jeremy Akins shortly before his death.

She knew Grampa would have written something that important down, either on a note or in his journal. She had found the journals he kept since his arrival in Alaska and read the most recent one, hoping for information she could use. He made no mention of selling or even loaning his prized dozer.

Without thinking, she raised the barrel of the shotgun as he started toward her with his fist raised. She didn't know whether he intended to strike her or not, but didn't want to find out. In his present condition, he might. His ruddy complexion paled visibly at the sight of the shotgun and he slowly lowered his hand. "Okay, you can take the dozer, I was just joking with you. You don't have to get violent about it."

As they neared the dozer, he motioned the operator to get down and she scrambled up the track and into the cab of the large machine. This wasn't too much different than the large tractor on the ranch, just a lever and pedal on each side to control the track on that side and steer, instead of a steering wheel. She would have to remember all that Grampa had written about running this machine so she could get it out of this place without having to ask for help. Luckily, the operator left the blade raised a bit above the ground and the engine running. Now, Grampa always kept a record of use in the tool box of the dozer, by the seat. He always wrote down the time on the hour meter, which was labeled, on the large dash with all the other instruments. She could tell by the numbers that Mr. Morse had used the dozer for quite some time. He watched her check the numbers and knew just what she was doing by the area she was looking at.

The shift was on the armrest and her left hand reached it quite comfortably when she sat down. It also was plainly labeled so should be no problem. She put the lever in reverse and slowly the dozer backed away from the pile of dirt. Stepping on the pedal and pulling the lever on her left, stopped the track turning on that side, so the dozer slowly turned, facing the road. She slid the lever to 1 and sure enough, the dozer started forward. Hey, this was easy. She didn't dare try speeding the engine up, she would probably go right through their old trailer house. Oh well, that would come later, the speeding up, not the going through the trailer.

After getting around several bends in the road, so no one could see if she made a mistake, she stopped and tried out the throttle and decelerator. On this type of dozer, the foot pedal was raised to speed up and lowered to slow down, just the opposite of a car. The throttle was set by hand for as fast or as slow as the top speed you wanted, then controlled by the foot pedal. This would definitely take some getting used to. The lever near her right hand was the blade control. She practiced raising and lowering it several times, it seemed easy enough. So setting the throttle at a bit higher speed than it had been, she eased into first gear and went home. Yes, the cabin was home now. She would make out okay.

Chapter 4

The next few days were spent getting caught up on sleep and getting herself oriented to her new life. She read more of Grampa's journals, they would be her best source of information. She found pamphlets and brochures from various State and Federal Agencies, explaining the permits needed and regulations that had to be followed to mine. Some of the regulations didn't seem to make much sense to her. A Miner was expected to return water to the stream clearer than most city drinking water, after having washed their pay dirt in it.

The charts complied from data by the U.S. Bureau of Mines, D.G.G.S., and from the Alaska Department of Fish and Game didn't coincide with the supposedly unbiased research done by other groups wanting more stringent regulations on mining. Putting the charts together clearly showed that most of the peak salmon harvest years coincided with the peak years of totally unregulated mining activity plus the recent upswing in mining after gold was deregulated. This didn't sound as though mining were ruining the fishing industry to her. Now she had a bit of ammunition for her disagreement with that self righteous fellow from the E.C.S.

The dozer was proving easier to operate than she had expected. She took it up to the workings and was practicing sculpting the old tailings into new contours. Grampa had a good supply of fuel on hand and she wouldn't have to worry about that for this summer, anyway.

She figured out the actual mining process from reading Grampa's descriptions of what he had been doing. She already had picked the first small nuggets from the old sluice box from her first try at mining. It was hard to believe that these small bright flakes were worth more than just baubles. They were extremely heavy for their size and her small sample bottle was already getting some weight to it.

The days continued hot and dry and her small creek was rapidly becoming a small trickle. Her water supply to mine with was dwindling to just ½ hour every 12 hours. Grampa had not had time to repair his old pump so the water could be reused and she was not sure enough of her mechanical abilities to attempt it, yet. She would have to, in the future, or hire it done. She just didn't have the money, now, to cover that. There was still money left in Grampa's bank account in Fairbanks, but she didn't want to draw it out, except in an emergency.

That water in the pond surely couldn't still be as cold as she remembered it being at her earlier swim. She would just have to test it again. It was so hot and she felt so sticky, even if she was only working ½ hour twice a day. She put her hand into the water and it did feel nice, not exactly warm, but nice and refreshing. So off came the clothes and into the water she dove. It was still far from warm, under that surface water. In fact, she felt almost as though she were reliving her last swimming experience when she saw the shadow on the water as she surfaced. Sure enough, there were those gorgeous blue eyes that had been haunting her dreams, both while sleeping and awake. It should be illegal for one man to look so good.

He could not believe his eyes. This was the first time he had come back to the pond since their last encounter and here she was, again, swimming. Did she actually do this every day? That water never truly got warm, no matter how inviting it looked. Or did it?

He didn't wait for an invitation, but pulled off his shirt and boots as he came down to the water. He dove in without hesitation, only to confirm his suspicions about the water's warmth and his sanity. Hadn't he done this once before? Would she be gone when he surfaced, this time? He surfaced about 5 feet from where she was treading water, with her hair about her like a veil.

She felt as though she were still in one of her dreams and it didn't matter what one did in a dream, did it? She would never have been so bold if this had been reality. In fact, she would have been in a panic. The cold water was forgotten as he slowly came toward her. He slowly reached out to touch her cheek with his hand.

"I just had to see if you were real." His words shattered her dream state and she began to feel the panic welling up inside her. What on earth was she doing, calmly letting some strange man touch her, especially in these circumstances. His lips gently closed over hers and reality faded again.

It was brought back to both of them abruptly as they sank in the water, both forgetting to continue treading water. The pond was only about 8 feet deep, but that was enough to send them both sputtering back to the surface. She headed for the bank with her clothes on it as soon as her feet touched bottom. Swimming as fast as she could, she had almost made it when a strong hand closed around her ankle.

"Oh no, you don't. No disappearing act this time. I want to talk to you." (Among other things) his mind added.

"Dad sent me over to see if we could work something out on the dozer. My name is Mike Morse. Dad said you threatened him with a gun when you came over and took the dozer. He's not sure whether or not to press charges. You do realize you could be in serious trouble?"

Somehow this wasn't how a fantasy was supposed to work, was it? It seemed almost as though he disliked her, and he didn't even know her.

"I did not threaten Mr. Morse. When he came toward me with his fist up, I was afraid he was going to hit me. I was carrying the shotgun for protection from the bears."

"Ha, there hasn't been a bear around here in a long time. That's a pretty flimsy excuse."

This was unbelievable, here she was, in nothing but long wet hair and a pair of flimsy panties and all he could do is talk about the dozer. He couldn't believe he was actually saying these things. Her lips had been so soft and warm, the contrast with the cold water was so great, he had felt under a spell.

She had a hard time making her mind believe this was the same person that had kissed her so wonderfully only minutes ago. Was her dozer the only attraction for him? Was he just like her ex-fiance? Just wanting what she could do for him or his family?

She slowly eased her ankle out of his grasp and now made good her dash up the bank to her clothes. She didn't even slow down as she scooped them up and the shotgun as she ran toward the cabin. As she dashed around the corner of the cabin, she ran headlong into Will Turner, the E.C.S. representative. To her chagrin, they ended in a heap in the grass by the cabin door. Mike Morse had taken the time to pull on his clothes but was not far behind her and rounded the corner just as she and Will were beginning to extricate themselves from their tangle. Again they went sprawling. Her hair was drying fast from her run to the cabin and the hot sun so covered her quite well in a rippling mantle. This was one time she was glad it was so long. It hid her face as well as the major portion of her body. Both of the men seemed mesmerized by it and each reached out a tentative hand to touch a stray strand. She still had a grip on the shotgun but had no idea where her clothes had scattered to. She whirled and slammed into the cabin, yanking the door shut behind her.

This was just too much. Not a soul shows up for days and now two men, at the worst possible timing. If these were her Prince Charmings she could probably do without their help. She felt bruised from one end to the other.

She refused to open the door, as they alternately pounded on it and glared at each other. Really, this must all be a bad dream and she would wake up pretty soon. She certainly hoped so, anyway.

She found some more clothes and dressed. Her hair was a mass of tangles and would take forever to straighten up. She started in, peeking out the window once in a while to see if the men had left yet or not. They stood back a ways and were conversing in low tones, at least she could not make out the conversation from in the cabin. Will spotted something in the edge of the road and they both bent down to look at it. Mike seemed a bit subdued as they turned and came back to the cabin. He knocked on the door, then spoke just loud enough for her to hear, "I owe you an apology, there is a bear around here. In fact, by the tracks, it has been here very recently and is very large. Please let us talk to you.."

She unlocked the door and stepped back, with the shotgun close at hand. The two men came into the cabin, Mike automatically ducked, he must have been in here before. When Grampa built the cabin, he saw no reason to make a door any taller than was necessary for his own convenience. Mike must be at least 2 or 3 inches taller than Grampa had been. She was 5'8" so had no problem. Will was about 5'10" or maybe a bit more, but Mike was at least 6'3".

Both men seemed a bit embarrassed and neither one seemed to know how to start a conversation with her. She did not make it easy for them, she just stood there waiting. Finally both started to say something, then stopped, started, stopped and glared at each other. This was definitely not the way a fantasy should go, although now that she stopped to think about it, this was the first time in her life that anyone ever had vied for her attention. Now she had two men standing here, looking like they would like to strangle each other, but she wasn't sure it was because of her or something else. Maybe they just didn't like each other and she wasn't too sure she liked either of them, either, right now.

She always bruised easily and now she could tell that there was a beauty on her cheek from her tumble into Will. Also some of her ribs felt tender. She knew her bottom would be black and blue from both falls and even her ankle felt swollen and sore from Mike's grip in the pond. Might as well make them both even more uncomfortable than they already were.

"If you two have something to say, please say it, so I can doctor my bruises in peace and quiet."

Both men turned and noticed her cheek for the

first time. Both turned accusing eyes on the other. Both spoke as one, "What did you do to her?"

She really didn't know how to cope with this and decided to try the delicate feminine act, or as much of one as she could bring herself to do.

"I'm sorry, you'll both have to leave. I have a terrible headache and I really do need to tend to these bruises. You'll just have to come back later, if you wish to talk to me."

Mike came over and gently led her to the couch, he helped her get comfortable while Will started a kettle of water heating on the gas stove. She was so startled by their sudden care and attention that she didn't think to ask what they thought they were doing.

This <u>was</u> rather nice, having two good looking men waiting on her. It was certainly something she had never experienced before. She was always the one that waited on the sick or injured members of her family and toughed out her own illness or injuries. Maybe there was something to be said for accepting a helping hand once in a while. She would have to think about this. Her threat of a headache seemed to be coming true. Her head was throbbing from the fall, she must have hit a rock, in the very least, to make the lump she felt from her cheek toward her ear.

Then she noticed that Will was also gingerly touching his head. She must have run into the back of his head but it had happened so fast she couldn't remember just how they had hit. For that matter,

Mike was starting to notice a few tender spots from the second collision. As she looked at them, then at herself, she started to laugh. Both men turned quickly toward her, not knowing if she was hysterical or what. She wondered herself, but figured it was probably or what.

"I'm sorry to laugh, but aren't we the gimpy looking bunch? I have more bruises than I care to think about and I would imagine both of you do, too. Yet here you both are, taking care of me. It's getting late and I am hungry. I have a large kettle of stew in the cooler, I can't seem to get the hang of cooking for just one. Would you like to have some dinner and we can discuss our business afterwards?"

Both men accepted, so she got the kettle of stew, made with some of the fresh vegetables from the garden, started heating. While it was getting hot, she made a quick batch of dumplings and dropped them onto the bubbling stew and covered it. The radio was on and soft music filled the silence as she worked. The men set the table while she fixed a small salad from more vegetables she picked earlier in the day.

The men ate in near silence, only asking for more and voicing their approval as they finished it off. She still had a couple of pieces of a cake made earlier in the week and had considered feeding to the Canadian Jays or Camp Robbers, earlier that day.

She didn't know where they were putting all that food, but she wouldn't have to worry about leftovers. Every crumb of the cake followed the stew, dumplings and salad. The cake was a chocolate fudge cake, split and filled with chocolate pudding between the layers. A whipped chocolate frosting covered it all and certainly satisfied her craving for chocolate. But after a couple of pieces, she totally lost her appetite for chocolate. She took some over to Harlan Henry's cabin, but he was not home at the time. She left it and hoped the animals or birds didn't get into it before he got home.

Will spoke first, after giving a satisfied sigh, "That was the best meal I have eaten in a long time. You should set up a restaurant somewhere, you'd make a fortune. I brought you some of our literature so you can read up on the damage being done to this beautiful State. I hope you will read it, it's very important."

"What damage are you talking about?" asked Mike.

"The irreparable damage being done to this State by mining, for one thing. The fisheries are being destroyed and the animal habitat, besides the scenery."

This was the opportunity she had been waiting for. Before Mike could answer, and she could tell by the way he was starting to look, that the brief truce was over, she jumped in. "I have some charts and date for you to read, too."

"Well, what is this, a meeting of the Greenies? Are you out here to spy on the rest of us? No wonder you stopped our mining the other day. You are one of "Them"." So saying, Mike stomped out of the cabin, not giving her a chance to explain.

Will sat there looking extremely pleased with himself. He was sure she was starting to see the truth of his statements. Thus, it was a shock to him when she launched into him, backed by the data from the various studies and reports she had read, plus Grampa's journal. He had never seen the charts from Fish & Game nor the ones from the D.G.G.S. or the Bureau of Mines.

This was even more of a shock, because he was so certain that he was in the right. This information was never discussed at any of their E.C.S. meetings. The final straw was the fact that all of the ground between Grampa's cabin and the airfield had been mined, once, several years ago. The overgrown mounds along the road were old tailing piles, with the trees and moss completely covering them. This was unbelievable. She showed him the early photos taken in the first gold rush to this area. Grampa collected quite a few and had a good selection of books from that era, also. Most of these were filled with photos and descriptions of the way the area had been mined.

When Will left, a couple of hours later, he was in a daze. This could not be true. If it was true, then he felt like a prize fool. What was it she had called him on their first meeting? A chauvinistic encephalitic simian? Maybe she wasn't too far off the mark. He wasn't too sure he liked that thought.

As he drove along the road, he looked at the overgrown mounds and tried to believe they were a natural part of the scenery. But since he had seen the photos and read parts of the books, he couldn't quite do it. Why, this area was beautiful and it had all been mined, already. The thought boggled his mind.

How was he going to explain this to the others in the E.C.S.? They were already looking to him as a strong leader in their movement.

Chapter 5

She sat at the table, trying to make some kind of sense of the last few hours. There was a light knocking at the door, she rushed over to open it. She expected Mike to return so she could talk to him, but the person at the door was not Mike. From her Grampa's description, this could only be Thaddeus Rory. He had some claims a bit farther over than Harlan Henrys and had also been one of Grampa's best friends.

"I heard that you were here, so thought I would stop over and introduce myself. I'm Thaddeus Rory, although most folks just call me Thad. You must be JoAnna. Jeremy always said you would come up here to live. He sure did set a lot of store by you, girl. Just wish he could see you here, at home, in this cabin. Well, maybe he does, at that. Heard you had a bit of disagreement with Cleve, he always was sort of heavy handed. No one will pay any attention to anything he says, unless it's that son of his. Mike knows what his father is like, but doesn't want to admit it, even to himself. Here, now, what happened to your cheek? Looks like you lost a fight with the door."

Well, a person would never have to worry about

the conversation as long as Thad was around. She stepped back and offered him a cup of coffee, her thoughts had turned to chocolate again and she started the oven preheating for a pudding cake. As Thad talked, she quickly mixed the cake in the pan, sprinkled the pudding ingredients on top, poured some boiling water on it and put it in the oven. Thad had been watching as he talked and now asked just what kind of thing she was making. Hadn't even seen anything like that before. When she told him the pudding would sink to the bottom and the cake would be on top when it was done, he snorted.

"What do you think, I'm someone you can fool easily? Cake don't do that."

She assured him that it would indeed do as she said. He didn't say any more on the subject, but when she removed the cake from the oven, she saw his eyes widen. The cake was on top. She spooned some into bowls an put some of the pudding on top. As soon as he tasted it, he sighed, "Ah, this is good. I've never seen anything like it and simple, too. Could I have your receipt?"

It took a moment to figure that he wanted the recipe, but then, that is what her great aunt always called them, too.

"Certainly, I'll write it down for you. Preheat your oven to 350 degrees. In an 8x8 inch pan, mix ¾ cup sugar, 1 ¼ cup flour, 2 tablespoons cocoa, 2 teaspoons baking powder and ½ teaspoon salt. Add 2 tablespoons oil, 1 tablespoon vanilla and 1 cup of milk and mix it well. Spread it evenly over the bottom of the pan. In a separate bowl, mix 1 ¾ cups brown sugar and ¼ cup cocoa. Sprinkle it over the cake batter, don't stir. Pour about 1 ½ cups boiling water over and still don't stir, put it in the oven and bake about 40 to 45 minutes. I like it best right out of the oven, but it is good, cold, also." and handed him the recipe.

"Thank you, Jo. I have enjoyed my visit with you very much and hope you will come over to my place soon. I'll certainly try out this receipt. Always did have a weakness for chocolate, also for nice wider ladies, too. Nothing personal, but you are just too young and you aren't a wider, are you ?"

Laughing, she assured him she was not yet a widow as she had never been married yet. He said his goodbyes and walked briskly down the road. He was whistling a merry tune and she thought he looked like a leprechaun as he stopped and did a few dance steps to his own tune. No wonder Grampa had liked him. She did, too.

The days passed swiftly as she learned how to mine. Harlan and Thad were steady visitors and gave her much needed advice. She would walk over and see them occasionally, also. They stopped by in an ancient Jeep and invited her to go with them to the little settlement about 30 miles away. She had gone and enjoyed herself very much. She was surprised to find a Post Office and a couple of letters for her. They were from Grampa's attorney and forwarding some mail he had received from her family and one from her ex-fiance, Bill.

She immediately scribbled out notes to her family with her correct general delivery mailing address at this Post Office and sent them out.

She was surprised the Postmaster held the mail for her, waiting for it to be picked up when she had not even let him know she was in the area. He assured her that everyone knew Jeremy's granddaughter was here. He knew it was just a matter of time before she would show up for the mail. She then wrote a note to the attorney, thanking him for sending her mail on to her. The offer to buy the property had also been renewed, in his letter. He advised her to consider it as it was very generous. She would wait until she got home, before she opened Bill's letter. She didn't want to possibly ruin the spirit of the day.

There was a pay phone outside the roadhouse on the wall of the building. She decided to call her folks to let them know she was okay. Her younger sister answered and immediately asked when she was coming home and how soon the wedding would be. Bill had let them in on the secret plans for their wedding and was she going to get married in Alaska or at home?

Jo didn't have the foggiest notion what Sue was babbling on about and told her so. She could tell her sister didn't believe her, but that was too bad. Her folks weren't home, but Sue wrote down the address and would assure them everything was okay.

Harlan and Thad insisted on buying her dinner at the roadhouse and then they spent the evening inviting everyone they knew that was in "town" to stop by for a drink and meet Jeremy's granddaughter. It had turned into quite a party and she was enjoying herself very much. Everyone was friendly and seemed to accept her immediately as one of them. She had never met such nice people, so willing to assume she was a nice person, also, until proven otherwise, if that were the case. It certainly was a different attitude than the one in her hometown area where everyone was treated like an outcast until they could prove otherwise, which sometimes took years. Some people never attained the status of being accepted, even her family, who were in the second generation in the area and still considered relative newcomers.

There was to be a huge party for the Fourth of July celebration and everyone made a point of inviting her to it. She was definitely looking forward to it, by the end of the evening. It had been a wonderful day.

Somehow, the time never seemed right to open Bill's letter, so it remained unopened, on the windowsill. Her garden was doing very well and she decided to fix something from the garden, maybe a huge salad, to take to the party on the Fourth. She would bake a cake and make some rolls, also. Maybe cheese rolls. She had found a can of dehydrated cheddar cheese in her food supply and it worked great, added to the bread dough.

She was still working on her claims, a little bit every day. Her sample bottle was getting a nice weight to it. Harlan suggested she clean up her sluice box before they went to "town" for the party. Once in a while there had been thievery from the boxes while everyone was gone. He came over and helped her, explaining each step as they went, so she could do it herself next time. There were several ounces of fine gold on the carpet under the riffles, when they were done. She had been excited to see just how much gold there was. There had been some pretty clear stones that she picked out of the box, also. They were not large, but she thought they were rather pretty and would add them to the growing collection of unusual rocks and stones she had been picking up ever since she got here. Harlan joked about her picking them up, saying maybe she had diamonds, too, as diamonds have been found in Alaska.

Added to the larger gold flakes and small nuggets she had been picking out of the box, the fine gold made a nice cleanup. Considering the fact that she did not work very much each day, she thought it was a fortune. Harlan weighed it for her and told her about what it would be worth if she sold it.

He recommended she try to get the pump fixed so she could work longer each day. She could live on what she was making, but only if she stayed out here in the cabin, not move into town for the winter. If she canned and dried vegetables from the garden and took care of the large assortment of berries as they ripened later in the summer, she would even make some money to save for the future. If she were lucky enough to kill a moose, she would really be set for the winter. He cautioned against killing a moose too early in the autumn because with no freezing facilities, the meat might not keep until freeze up.

She spent the afternoon baking for the party the next day. She gathered some of the vegetables for a salad but would pick the lettuce early in the morning so it would be fresh and crisp.

Bill's letter still sat accusingly on her windowsill. The time just never seemed right to open it. She could almost look at their engagement as just another learning experience. She had learned a great deal from it and hoped to never repeat the experience. He was an extremely conceited individual and thought the whole world should revolve around him. She was just glad she had not given in and married him. Her sister thought she was crazy for breaking up with him and told her so, often. She suspected her folks thought the same, but were too fond of her to tell her so.

She still had not gone to Fairbanks for fresh supplies. There was so much food on hand, she really hadn't missed anything. She found flour, powdered eggs, powdered milk and the garden was getting into full swing. She would soon have to buy some canning jar lids. Grampa had lots of canning jars and a dandy pressure canner, but only a few lids on hand. She still needed some rubber boots, her sneakers were getting seriously raggedy and so were her jeans. Scrubbing them on an old washboard wasn't helping them either. She should get some winter clothes. Grampa's could be used, but were too large. She would use his fur parka and the insulated pants could be shortened and taken in a bit. The boots were the problem. They were just way too big. She would walk right out of them.

She baked the cake while waiting for the rolls to finish raising and was just taking the cake out of the oven when there was a knock at her door. She did not know the man standing there. He introduced himself as George Watson, and explained that he was the representative of the company interested in buying her property.

She invited him in and returned to putting the large pan of rolls in the oven. She fixed him a cup of coffee while she continued to work on the food for the party the next day. She explained to him that she was not interested in selling and thought her two earlier refusals made that point abundantly clear.

She was sorry he made the trip out here for nothing, but she was not selling. He seemed to think she was just holding out for more money. He could not believe she was seriously considering staying here and mining by herself. He seemed quite upset by her refusal to even consider his offer and started making thinly veiled innuendoes about the line of business she must be in and the possibility of accidents happening to people by themselves.

He even had the gall to suggest that her Grampa would still possibly be alive if he had listened to reason and sold. That was too much. She was trying to be nice and this jerk was taking the sale refusal personally and she was feeling threatened by his attitude. But she felt real fear when he stood up and started around the table towards her. The look of hatred on his face was definitely out of proportion to her refusal to sell her property.

She backed toward the dish drainer, she had left a large butcher knife upright in the corner of the drainer when she washed up, earlier. He didn't notice her hand slowly reaching behind her for the knife, when he suddenly lunged at her. She gripped the knife and put it between them. His forward motion carried him right into the point of the knife. The knife sank about 2 inches into the flab of his belly. His eyes bulged at the sight of his own blood starting to well around the little cut. Although the knife had pushed in about 2 inches, he was so flabby and fat that there was only a small break in the skin. His white shirt would definitely need replaced and the suit would probably need cleaned, but he wouldn't even need a stitch. Maybe a Band-Aid.

The sight of his own blood seemed to take all the hostility out of him, for the moment. He looked at his stomach then at her with a horrified expression. "You're crazy, that's what you are, a crazy woman. You ought to be locked up somewhere. You just tried to kill me."

"No, Mr. Watson, I did not try to kill you. If I had, you would now be dead, not standing there looking like an imbecile. Now get out of my home and don't ever come back. I shall definitely inform your home office of your tactics and shall consider you a threat if I ever see you on my property again. The next time I find you here, I shall shoot on sight."

At her mention of informing his employers, he seemed to shrink in size and bluster.

"Oh, come on now, " he whined, "I didn't intend you any harm. I just wanted to show you how vulnerable a young woman alone out here really is. I wasn't going to hurt you."

She really didn't know if she would actually carry out her threat to shoot him, but she wanted him to think she would.

"If you aren't out of my house in 3 seconds, I shall reconsider my options and shoot you here and now."

So saying, she picked up the shotgun but he was already out the door. He stalled the engine of his car three times, trying to get it turned around and out of her yard. Every time he happened to glance in her direction, he would stall it, so she stepped back into the cabin. The man definitely had a problem. She hoped she would never see him again.

Her cheese rolls almost baked too long, but were still okay. She had forgotten them while talking to Mr. Watson. Her head was still spinning from all the things he said and hinted at.

Could Grampa's death actually be the result of some kind of arranged accident? She just assumed it to have been a heart attack or old age, but Grampa was always so careful and his health was good, too. She would have to start asking questions. Harlan and Thad would the best ones to start with. She would ask them tomorrow on their way to the celebration.

Chapter 6

The next morning was clear and bright. She picked and cleaned the lettuce and fixed the other vegetables for the salad. She just finished the dressing and poured it into a jar to take with them when Harlan and Thad showed up in the ancient Jeep. She carried the box of goodies to the Jeep and went back for her purse and to lock up the cabin. It was unusual to lock doors, here, but after Mr. Watson's visit. She had lost her feeling of safety.

On the ride to the little settlement, she told the men about Mr. Watson and what he had said. She did not omit a single detail. When she finished, Harlan stopped the Jeep and sat looking at her. Both he and Thad looked about half sick.

"No, now I don't know what to think. I always did think Jeremy was too careful around equipment to pull a stupid stunt like the one he died from. We got to go to Fairbanks in a couple of days and talk to the State Troopers. This is serious business, Jo. Would you like to come with us?"

"I have been planning on going, so yes, I would like to go in with you, if you are sure it isn't going to be too much trouble for you. I only saw the International Airport and not much of that. So I have no idea of where to go or who to see. I would appreciate your help."

They were a rather subdued group when they arrived at the party. But it was hard to remain so, in the jubilant atmosphere of the celebration. Fireworks were a normal part of the day, but there would be no display in the evening as it was never dark this time of year. She found that most of the people saved the pretty rockets and such for New years Eve. No chance of fire with all of the snow and only 3 hours of daylight a day at that time of year made it perfect to celebrate with firework displays. She bought a bunch of rockets and roman candles to save.

No one even noticed the small plane until it was taxiing up near the little store. Jo was talking to some of her new acquaintances and just happened to glance up as a familiar figure was climbing out of the plane. No, it couldn't be, What on earth would Bill Humphries, her ex fiance, be doing here? Maybe if she closed her eyes, he would go away. That didn't work and pinching herself so hard she knew there would be a bruise later, didn't work either.

There he was, walking over in her direction. He stopped and asked a couple of people something and they helpfully pointed in her direction. She knew he must be here because of her. Maybe something had happened to her family, maybe she should at least talk to him instead of following her first instinct which was to run as fast as she could in

the opposite direction. He was accepting offers of
drinks as he made his way toward her. He never
drank around her family, but she knew he did drink
heavily once in a while. Today looked like it was
going to be one of those whiles.

When he reached her, he dropped his bag and
grabbed her in a tight embrace, kissing her soundly.
Was this actually Bill? He never liked public displays
of emotion, saying it was cheap. He stepped back
and looked at her with an odd gleam in his eyes.
Swinging around but still hanging onto her arm, he
announced their forthcoming marriage. Her mouth
popped open and she screamed, "NO WAY, YOU
JERK"

Now it was his turn to stand openmouthed. What
had come over her? He was counting on her
reticence and good manners to not let her oppose
him in public. Not only was she opposing him, she
actually called him a jerk. This was not going the
way he planned, at all. Maybe he should just marry
the little waitress he had been keeping. But Jo would
have all that lovely money, when her claims were
sold. She also was a hard worker and knew how to
run a ranch. Why shouldn't he marry her and keep
the waitress, too? It seemed like such a nice plan,
back at home.

He talked to that nice Mr. Watson in Fairbanks
and between them, they had planned the perfect way
to convince her to sign the papers he had in his
matched luggage. Of course, he was unable to find
Mr. Watson yesterday, in Fairbanks, but they

discussed it on the phone, before. Mr. Watson sent all the papers needing her signature and assured him he would receive a fair cut, besides her entire share, if everything worked out okay.

She had stalked off, not even asking him how his trip had been. She found Harlan and Thad with a group of their old buddies. They were about ready to leave and figured a bit earlier wouldn't hurt a thing. Someone would return her large salad bowl to her later. As they were pulling out, Bill came running over, "Hey, where do you think you are going? Let me get my bags, I'm coming with you."

"Like hell you are, don't come anywhere near me. I don't have a thing to say to you. It was all said before I came up here. You might just as well get back on that plane and go home."

Harlan put the Jeep in gear and left him in a cloud of dust.

"You don't much like that fellow, do you?" Thad asked innocently. "Never heard you use a cuss word before. How many more do you know?"

She couldn't help smiling at Thad. He really was a dear. Why were the only men she liked and got along with, too old? Mike was at the party but avoided her. She hadn't seen Will since the night she informed him of some of the often overlooked facts instead of fancies involving the mining and environmental concerns.

But it was hard to remain depressed around Thad. And Harlan was doing his best to cheer her up, too. By the time they reached her cabin, she was in good spirits again and ready to face whatever tomorrow might bring.

What tomorrow brought was not any better. The dozer wouldn't start and she spent several hours trying to figure out the problem, to finally find a rag stuffed in the air intake. When she got the dozer running and made her daily "splash" she parked the dozer behind her cabin. Maybe she would hear someone fooling around with it, there. When she checked the sluice box, there were large boot tracks around the box and some of the riffles appeared to have been checked. She was glad Harlan had advised her to clean the box the day before they went to town.

When they went to Fairbanks this afternoon, she would try to make it look as though she were still here. Maybe whoever was fooling around would be fooled, themselves. She decided to ask Harlan and Thad about getting a dog or cat. Either animal would let her know if someone were outside. Maybe get a dog and a cat. Maybe a husky so he could be an outdoor dog and a cat to keep her company in the cabin.

Chapter 7

Harlan and Thad pulled into her yard just a bit past noon. They had decided to go all out and left the Jeep at home. Thad had an elegant old Cadillac and they were going to Fairbanks in style.

The car was made before oil shortages and was built for luxury. Even though the highway was only a dirt and gravel road, they rode along in ease, hardly feeling the bumps and potholes.

Thad said he had been driving this road so long and often that he was on a first name basis with each and every bump and rock. The road looked like it was built, following the line of least resistance. It dipped into small valleys and followed ridge tops, They saw a cow and calf moose and a bit farther, a large grizzly bear. Both men voiced concern for the calf moose, saying the bears ate far more of them than the wolves did.

The ride to Fairbanks took about 3 hours and she was surprised by the size of the town. Since the airport is a few miles from town, she had seen none of it before.

They rented rooms at a hotel as soon as they got to Fairbanks and she called Grampa's attorney. He agreed to see her the following morning and they could talk, then.

Harlan and Thad decided she needed the grand tour of Fairbanks and took her everywhere they thought she might possibly be interested in. They bemoaned the loss of "2 Street", the section of Second Avenue that had been small bars in buildings from the Gold Rush days. They told stories of the goings on from the pipeline days that had spelled doom for "2 St." Evidently the city fathers thought Fairbanks could do without that bit of local color.

This issue was brought before the voters twice and voted down both times, but city fathers, thinking they were doing the right thing, had proceeded to buy up, force out of business and tear down, all the old buildings. Now the core downtown area was a mass of parking lots and new hotels. Now no one wanted to go check out 2 Street, nothing was happening there. Everyone shopped at the little malls sprouting up like mushrooms around the outskirts of town. She could see for herself that the downtown area was missing something. Thad claimed it had been killed, murdered and dissected. He thought the city should reconstruct the old buildings and make a historical bar row, or at least little gift shops if they didn't want all the drunks. On that note, they decided it was time for dinner.

As they were being served, she happened to glance at the door just as Will was coming in and the young woman with him was very pretty. He was looking down at the her smiling face and said something that removed the smile from her face.

The woman suddenly looked like she wanted to cry. Jo wondered if he were being his usual know-it-all self, and felt immediate pity for her. Will happened to look her way and jumped as he saw the scowl in her eyes and the look on her face. He flushed and hurriedly pulled the unresisting young woman with him to the other side of the restaurant.

He was talking earnestly to her as they sat down and soon she smiled at him, although not as brightly as before. He must have been very persuasive, because by the time they were served, she ate a very hearty meal. Jo, Harlan and Thad left soon after and Will did not come over to say Hi.

From the restaurant, they went to a bar that had a fairly good band. Several fellows asked Jo to dance and she enjoyed the evening very much. It was quite late by the time they said goodnight and went their separate ways at the hotel.

As she slid the keycard into the lock on her door, a hand fell on her shoulder. The grip was hard, not friendly and she immediately stepped back, hard, on the instep of the person behind her. She whirled around on her high heel point, still on his instep, swinging her purse soundly into the side of his head and bringing her knee up into his groin. As he collapsed into a moaning heap on the floor by her now open door, she saw that it was Will Turner. He didn't know what portion of his anatomy hurt the worst and lay curled in a fetal position, one hand over his head, the other holding his foot. Now, what the devil did he want?

Earlier in the day, Harlan and Thad decided she needed something smaller than her shotgun for carrying around, and bought her a small handgun at a garage sale they spotted on their sightseeing tour. She pulled it out of her bag and waited for Will to recover enough to tell her why he was here and what he wanted.

Right at that moment, Will couldn't really remember just why he had wanted to talk to her. Damn, why wasn't she like most women? He usually could talk most women into just about anything. That was the trouble, he never actually had time to talk, before she lit into him, either literally or figuratively. He certainly wasn't getting anywhere with the macho approach. He seemed to remember thinking that he would swing her around into his arms and kiss her into submission. She would invite him into her room, they would spend a pleasant night together, he would have her out of his system and could forget about her.

She haunted his dreams and had ruined his standing in the Environmental Conservation Society since their last conversation. He had asked about some of the things she brought to his attention and found out they were indeed the truth. The E.C.S. didn't take kindly to having some of their pet projects questioned and found lacking in truth. He was treated with all the warmth of a leper at a nudist colony at the meetings, now.

"Okay, Will. What do you want?"

"To be honest with you, right now, I don't know."

he gritted out. "I was going to talk to you about our last conversation, you were right, on everything you told me. I'm sorry if I startled you."

"Yes, you did scare me. I had a bad experience a couple of days ago and I didn't know it was you or what you wanted. I didn't mean to hurt you this much, but don't ever grab me that way again."

He didn't think she would have to worry about him grabbing her any way, at least not in the near future. What on earth did women pack in their purses, anyway,? Why weren't they required to register them as lethal weapons? Her knee should be registered, too, Maybe he should seriously consider the life of a monk. Maybe he would have to. He didn't think he had ever had such pain, even when he broke his arm when he was a kid. His foot was throbbing and as he tried to stand, it refused to accept his weight. He collapsed again, on the floor.

She considered leaving him there for housekeeping to find. But she decided it wouldn't look too good to have a fellow curled in a fetal position outside her door all night. There was a couch in her room, he could sleep on that. She pulled him into her room and helped him onto the couch. There was a spare blanket at the foot of her bed, so she tossed that over him. She went to the ice machine and brought him a bag of ice to use as he saw fit.

One of his eyes would be black and blue by morning and maybe a small bone broken in his foot. She wouldn't even think about what else might be bruised. There were extra plastic bags, he could make three ice packs from them. She suggested this and went into the bathroom to change for bed. She hadn't seen the need to bring a robe and didn't own a nighty, so T-shirt and sweat pants were it, it would have to do.

He studiously ignored her as she came out and went to bed. Damn, he had expected to spend the night with her, but this didn't fit the scenario he had planned. She wasn't even his type. He liked small fluffy girls that adored him. She was not that small, nor fluffy and it would be safe to say, she did not adore him. So what was the attraction he could not ignore? He followed her suggestion about the ice packs and after the initial shock of the cold, they were very soothing. He dozed off to sleep, only to waken as a cold trickle of water escaped the ice pack. He retied the bag and was soon asleep again. He didn't waken until after she was up and dressed. She asked if he could walk now and he found that he could.

As she opened her door and was helping him out, Mike came around the turn in the hall. He abruptly stopped and turned back the way he had came. The look of disgust on his face told her what he was thinking. Why did he always have to show up at the worst possible moments? What was he doing in Fairbanks? Will was watching her face and couldn't explain the feelings gong through him at her apparent interest in Mike. He would just have to keep reminding himself that she wasn't his type.

As he went down the hall with her helping him, he discovered that he wouldn't have to be a monk after all. What a time to find that out. Spend all night in her room, sleeping on the couch, of all things and now, out in the hall, find that he still wanted her. If this was one of life's little ironies, he could do without them.

She was so warm and was pressed against him so nicely as she helped him along. Before he embarrassed himself, he had better try walking on his own. He stopped and she turned her face inquiringly toward him. He couldn't resist, he kissed her surprised lips gently but with a wealth of feeling. It was even better than he had thought it would be. Now why had he done that? Now he certainly would not forget her as he planned and she still was not his type.

She stepped back from him. What did he think he was doing? He wasn't her dream man. Not even close. But the feel of his lips seemed to be burned on her lips. The urge to turn back to her room was almost overpowering. After his reception last night, he would think she was completely out of her mind if she were to suggest it. So would she.

They continued to the lobby, carefully not touching each other, each one longing to go back to her room. Each thinking the other would be offended if it were suggested.

Thad and Harlan were waiting for her in the lobby, both looked surprised to see Will with her.

"I thought Mike was going to get you. We talked

to him last night. He has the room next to mine and was just coming in as I got there, so we came down and had a couple of drinks and talked a while. He has some funny notion that you are a Greenie, Jo. Now where would he get a fool notion like that?" Thad asked.

The mention of Mike brought her back to reality, again. How could she even consider going to her room with Will? Mike, with the gorgeous eyes, was the perfect answer to her fantasies. "I'm not sure, Thad, he sure has acted odd. He wouldn't let me explain anything to him and I'm afraid that this morning hasn't improved things at all."

Will figured he better excuse himself and leave before she started telling them about last night's fiasco. He was uncomfortable enough without these two giving him a bad time about his intentions. He just knew they could tell what he wanted just by looking at him. So, with a sheepish grin, he excused himself and told Jo he would like to see her later while she was in town. Maybe they could go out to dinner or something.

After Will left, she explained what had happened last night, sort of. Harlan and Thad laughed and said she did the right thing, considering George Watson's actions the other day.

Chapter 8

After breakfast, they went to see Grampa's attorney. He was waiting for them and treated Thad and Harlan as old friends. She found herself liking him immediately. He was very distinguished looking, with wavy silver hair and a personality that invited confidences. She could see that would be an asset in a Court room.

She told him of George Watson's visit and innuendoes about her Grampa and the possibility of an "accident" befalling herself. She had worried that he would laugh at her fears, but he took them very seriously.

He told her he would have to do some questioning around town and would get back to her with anything he found. He also mentioned that Bill Humphries stopped in to see him and was representing himself as her agent in selling her property. Jo left no doubt in Steve Mathews' mind about Bill Humphries and his capacity as her agent.

Just wait until she saw Bill again. That fellow would have to learn that when she told him no, she meant no, not maybe.

Before they left Steve Mathews' office, it was arranged that he would send a letter to the company that George Watson represented and protest his methods and ask for him to cease bothering Jo Atkins. The property was not for sale, never had been.

It was decided to spend one more night in Fairbanks. Harlan and Thad both liked movies and there was quite a selection to choose from. It had been a very long time since she enjoyed herself as much as she did in the two men's company. Talking to Mr. Mathews seemed to lift a weight from her shoulders and she enjoyed the rest of the day tremendously.

They were like three children, let loose on the town with a car, enough money to do as they pleased as long as their tastes ran to the simple. They went to Alaskaland/Pioneer Park and through the Pioneer Museum. She enjoyed seeing the old relics from the Gold Rush Days, Thad said he took that personally.

They went to the Museum at the University of Alaska and she was impressed by the variety of the exhibits. Harlan said the old Museum had a much better gold exhibit. It was in a room of it's own, with mural paintings depicting the old-time methods of mining.

From the original story of the golden fleeces, which is the way they actually did mine way back then, using sheep hides instead of rugs in the bottom of the sluice boxes to catch the finer gold. Then the sheep hides were dried by draping them over bushes so the gold could be beat out of them later.

As she met Harlan and Thad in the lobby to go to dinner, Will came up to them. "May I take you out to dinner?"

Thad said he couldn't remember the last time he had been on a date and promptly accepted.

Will's face was a sight at this. He had had eyes only for Jo as he came in the lobby and hadn't expected the two old men to accompany them. Why didn't things ever go as he planned, where she was concerned?

She decided Thad was enjoying himself too much for her to turn down Will's offer of dinner. So the four of them went out to dinner. Will's little compact car was parked at the curb and the old men decided they would suffer possible terminal injury trying to ride in it and they all would fit in the old Caddy.

The two cars looked like David and Goliath and many remarks were made about the old car. Thad escorted Jo to the front seat, Harlan to drive and Thad shared the backseat with Will. Will did not think he was going to enjoy this evening at all. It was surprising to realize, later, that he was actually having fun. The two old men were great story tellers and Jo had a few of her own to add. He even found that he could tell a few. After dinner, they proceeded to the theatre and watched a movie that the two old men decided was unfit for human consumption. They decided against watching another one, so went instead to a night club that had a good band. There was a good crowd and dancing, so they ended up having a very good evening. Will asked Jo to dance with him as the music turned to a slow song. As they moved across the floor, she spotted the young woman Will had been with the evening before. Will spotted her about the same time and Jo felt him stiffen. Of course, what was she thinking? He was only using her until his girlfriend forgave him for their little tiff. She was overdoing it a bit though, by being with another guy and letting him paw her in such a manner. Jo couldn't believe it, Will abandoned her on the dance floor and walked over to the other woman and her escort. Jo went back to her table and had just asked Thad and Harlan if they would mind taking her back to the motel when Will came back to their table, dragging the unwilling young woman behind him.

"This is my sister, Lorraine. Mom sent her up here, thinking I could influence her, but as you can see, she still does whatever she pleases. Could I impose on you to give us a ride back to my car? I'm sorry Jo, I shouldn't have left you on the dance floor like that. It was very rude of me. But Lorraine was supposed to be staying with a girlfriend tonight. I just don't know what to do. I can't just lock her in her room although that's what I'd like to do, right at this minute. Sorry to end the evening like this."

Thad sat in the back, talking to the sullen young woman, on their way back to the hotel. Lorraine had brightened perceptively by the time they reached it. Jo wondered what Thad said to her to make such a difference in her manner. Well, it was none of her business and she would probably never see either one of them again anyway. But at least it had been his sister, instead of another girl that he had left her. Seen up close, the girl looked about 15 or 16. The fellow she had been with looked about 30. He was a rough looking man and she did not see what Lorraine had seen in him. He was drinking heavily and treating her roughly. Jo thought Lorraine was secretly pleased to be hauled out of the club by her brother. Jo knew she would have been, in the circumstances. How had the girl even gotten in to the bar? She was made up to look older, but was still just a kid. Oh well, it was still none of her business.

As they were saying goodnight at the hotel, Will asked if he could see her again, sometime. "I actually enjoyed myself this evening, even if it wasn't at all what I planned. I'm sorry my sister showed up with that fellow. He seems to egg her on and I don't know how to cope with it. I'm going to have to send her back to Mom and she don't know what to do, either."

The evening hadn't been what Jo planned, either, but she, too, had enjoyed herself. Except for that brief burst of - - - was it actually jealousy? Now why would she be jealous of anyone Will showed attention to? It couldn't be. She was only upset because he left her on the dance floor. That was it, she wasn't jealous. She told him sure, stop by her cabin any time he was in the area.

That still wasn't exactly what he had meant but it was better than a flat refusal to ever see him again. He would be sure to stop at her cabin. Maybe that would be a better idea after all. There wouldn't be all the distractions that seemed to crop up in town. Maybe tomorrow, no, that would be a little obvious. Just what was the attraction he felt for her? She still wasn't his type.

Harlan and Thad gently teased her about Will as they went down the hall to their rooms. They escorted her to her door and waited until she checker her room for boogeymen, they continued teasing. But she was glad of their concern for her well being. They would come by for her, early, have breakfast, then go back to the creeks.

The trip back was uneventful and they only saw grouse and rabbits along the road.

Chapter 9

Everything was peaceful looking as they pulled up in front of her cabin. It had been a nice change, to go to town, but it was heavenly to be home again. They had stopped at a grocery store just before leaving Fairbanks and stocked up on fresh goods and bug repellant. It would be nice to have fresh eggs for a while. Powdered eggs were okay, but there is no way to have them over easy or boiled. Luckily, she liked omelets and scrambled eggs.

Someone had picked up her mail at the little Post Office on the river bank and left it in a plastic bag between the screen door and the main door. There were some letters from her mother and one from her sister. Harlan told her when anyone went to "town" everyone's mail was picked up and brought out. That way, each and every person didn't have to go in each week for mail. It saved time and fuel.

Her whole family seemed to still think she was going to marry Bill. She would have to think of a final way to convince them that she was not now or ever in the future, going to marry Bill. Just what had he told them, anyway? After her next letter home, there should be no doubt in their minds as to her feelings for Bill. How could she ever have considered marrying such a pompous, self centered jerk? What a narrow escape she had made. To think, at one time she even considered herself rather lucky that he expected her to marry him. It was amazing how one's point of view could change so, in a few weeks.

As she sat, trying to compose the letter to end her parents delusions about her ever marrying Bill, there was a small tapping at her door. She had not heard any vehicles on the road. Now who could it be? One way to find out would be to answer the door, so she did.

Lorraine!

Now how on earth had she gotten here? For that matter, what was she doing here?

"May I come in? Please?"

"Oh. Yes, excuse me. I just wasn't expecting to see you here. Is everything okay? How did you get here?"

"I'm okay. I hitch-hiked out from Fairbanks. I started early this morning and hid in the brush along the road when I saw your car coming. Then it was quite a while before anyone else picked me up. A nice fellow that lives a few miles beyond the airstrip let me off there and told me how to get here. He said it was only a mile or so, but I think it's a lot farther than that."

"I know the feeling. I flew out here, the first time and walked up here from that airstrip. I didn't think I was ever going to find the cabin. But does your brother know where you are? Isn't it dangerous to hitch-hike?"

"Well, yes, it isn't a good idea to hitch-hike but I didn't know of any other way to get out here. Will was going to send me back to my Mom. She's a wonderful person and I love her very much, but since Dad died, she has had a rough time. I'll admit, I didn't help, but I miss him too. May I please stay with you a while? I'll help out and work with you, please? I wrote Will a note and dropped it in the mail. He'll get it in the morning. It'll be okay. He just wants to get rid of me, so I've done it for him and without having to move in with that jerk I was with the other night."

"If the guy was such a jerk, why did you keep going out with him?"

"He seemed like a nice guy when I first met him. He thought I was special and it's been a long time since anyone treated me like I was anything more than just a pest. So I went out with him. Then, it got to be just to spite Will. I guess that was sort of stupid, too, but at the time it seemed like the thing to do."

Jo couldn't help it, she liked Lorraine. The woman didn't seem to be a bad person, just someone that needed a helping hand. Well, she always did have a soft spot n her heart for anything or anyone that needed help.

"Okay, you can stay a while. I really don't have much to do, but the garden is starting to produce and you can help me with that. Do you mind sleeping on the couch?"

"Jo, right now, I wouldn't mind sleeping on the floor. I bet I actually walked almost as much as I rode on the way out here. I kept expecting Will to pull up and drag me back. I will be 18 next month, but he still thinks of me as a baby. I love it up here in Alaska and want to stay. At least a full year so I can see what winter is like. I would love to get my own place and go back to school."

"Grampa always had high praise for the University at Fairbanks. He wanted me to come up and go to school there. My folks just couldn't see letting me come up here, even though Grampa said he would get a place in town for us. I've always wished I could have done it."

Lorraine had brought a small backpack full of clothes, so they found a few pegs for the things that needed hung up. They laughed about their skimpy wardrobes. Both girls tended to wear jeans, T-shirts and sweatshirts with sneakers. Jo had one dress and the nice slack set she traveled up in. Lorraine stuck in one sun dress but forgot shoes. She brought several bottles of rather potent bug repellant. Jo figured she wasn't all fluff if she could think of the necessities like that.

The women talked late into the night, not paying attention to the time as it was light all night. So they slept in the next day. Jo was fixing a late breakfast or early lunch and Lorraine was weeding in the garden when a vehicle pulled up in the yard. Jo had just reached the door when Will banged on it.

"Where's Lorraine? Is she okay? I should have expected something like this, all she could talk about was you, after we left the hotel the other night. I'll kill her."

"I'm glad to see you too and won't you come in?" Jo said sweetly.

Will stopped. "I'm sorry, that girl drives me around the bend. But is she here and okay?"

"Yes, to both questions. She's out in the garden now, so I would like to talk to you about her a minute. It's okay with me if she stays here a while, if is okay with you. But make her ask. I think she needs another female, close to her age, to talk to. She seems to think I know all the answers, so a little time here should disabuse her of that notion. But it will also give her some time to stop and think out what she is going to do with the rest of her life. She really can't stand the guy she was out with the other night. But she does some of these things because she thinks she has to show her independence. Maybe she can find a different form of independence out here."

"Would you really put up with her for a while? She can be a real pain in the a…neck."

"That's funny, she says the same thing about you. Maybe a little time away from each other will improve your mutual opinions."

Jo added a bit more to the meal she was fixing, invited Will to stay and called Lorraine. As soon as Lorraine found that Will was not going to immediately haul her off, she relaxed. The meal wasn't exactly over run with hilarity, but no one committed any acts of bodily harm, either. Jo considered it a success.

Lorraine actually told Will she was sorry for running off as she had and asked permission to stay with Jo. Will figured anyone that could have enough influence on Lorraine to actually get her to behave in this manner and after only part of one day, should have her indefinitely. He didn't say this to Jo, but did give his permission for Lorraine to stay. He told them he would be back in the area in about a week. He would bring fresh supplies and a few more clothes for Lorraine. He would also see if Jo had changed her mind about Lorraine staying.

After he left, the women went out to the dozer and started it up. Jo didn't find any evidence of tampering, this time, and they were soon on their way up to the cut. She mentioned the rag in the air intake to Harlan. He said that sometimes some of the environmental groups sabotaged equipment, thinking they were "saving" the land. They didn't realize this whole area was mined less than 50 years before and was now so beautiful they thought it was virgin wilderness. The men both said she was lucky it was only a blocked air intake as some people had their equipment destroyed. She didn't feel all that lucky at the time, but would have been out of business for good if the dozer had been ruined.

She would have to find a way to lock the metal panels that kept brush out of the engine compartment and lock the fuel cap, also. She would have to find someone to weld for her and maybe teach her a bit about welding, too. Grampa had a small welder in the shed the pickup was in. She needed to find out what supplies were needed, maybe most of it was already here. She would probably find a book teaching welding on the bookshelves. Grampa had a good supply of self help books on almost any subject. She could get an education, right here. Maybe she should start a systematic study of all of Grampa's books. Maybe Lorraine would like to join her. They could always get more books for subjects not covered and study up on their weak subjects. There were tests to be taken to earn the equivalent of two years of college. They would have to look into that.

The next week passed quickly. The women fell into a routine of working together that suited them both. Lorraine weeded in the garden while Jo cooked breakfast. After eating, they went up to the cut and made the daily short mining shift.

The weather stayed warm and dry, so there wasn't much water for each day's working. The gold in Jo's bottle was adding up to a nice heavy weight for the size of the bottle. Not as much as it would have been if she had been able to get the pump running to recirculate the water so she could mine as many hours per day as she felt up to. Maybe the pump repair would be her winter project. Oh, so her subconscious was already planning the winter for her, was it? Well, she would have to consider it some more.

Lorraine's main problem seemed to be not having someone that would really listen to what she needed to say. Her mother was so wrapped in her own grief that she couldn't give Lorraine the time and attention required to help them both through this difficult time. Will had not been living at home, only there for short visits, for over 5 years, and really didn't feel the loss so keenly. Or maybe he just had a different way of handling it. He certainly didn't want to discuss it with Lorraine, although talking about it might have helped them both understand one another more.

Jo's loss of her grandfather helped her understand the grief and need to talk about it, that Lorraine felt. So they usually talked about their recent losses while they both worked in the garden or picked the wild berries that were starting. The wild blueberries were just starting to ripen, and Jo wanted to have plenty for later use. She canned several quarts for pies, made jam and jelly and dried some for adding to muffins or pancakes.

Grampa had a note in one of his journals about a way to preserve the blueberries by putting a layer of sugar in a crock or gallon jar, then a layer of berries, sugar and berries to the top of the container, topping with sugar. Cover lightly and just dip out what was needed, as needed. Keep in a cool place and try to use before warm weather started the berries fermenting in the spring. There were also recipes for wild berry liqueurs and wines made from the pulp after making the liqueur, and added notes saying it was extremely potent. The low bush cranberry or lingonberry made a great liqueur and also could be used as a cough syrup or for flu. Jo decided to try all these new things and see which ones she liked, for future use.

The women were not expecting Will to show up as soon as he did. They were in the middle of baking a blueberry pie when he came to the door. He could not believe that his sister was actually learning to bake. Jo had made a pie a couple of days before and they took it over to Harlan's cabin. Thad was there, so they made a small party out of the occasion. So Lorraine was trying her hand at making one today with Jo's supervision.

The pie came out of the oven a beautiful golden brown and smelled heavenly. Will could hardly wait for it to cool enough to cut. He had ice cream in a cooler in the car so was bribing the girls to cut the pie when Thad and Harlan showed up and the afternoon passed in a general mood of fun.

The pie turned out beautifully and disappeared with great rapidity. Mike stopped by when he saw Harlan's Jeep out front. It was the first time Jo had seen him since that disastrous morning at the hotel in Fairbanks. He seemed rather stiff at first, but soon relaxed and entered into the spirit of fun. It would have been hard for him not to, with Thad's puckish sense of humor and leprechaun grin. Harlan had a harmonica in his pocket and entertained them all with his playing. They all joined in singing some of the songs and sounded very good to themselves. They decided they should do this at least once a week, so it was decided same place, same time, next week. Will asked if anyone needed anything brought out from town and several small items were mentioned.

Mike still didn't know what to think of Will. He knew he worked for an environmental group, but everyone seemed to accept him, now, as one of the group. For his part, Will didn't seem to be such a know-it-all as he had, at the start.

Will now felt a bit ashamed of his previous attitude. He also felt extreme frustration at the way his relationship with Jo was progressing, actually not progressing. He was more attracted to her than ever and she still wasn't his type. She was almost as tall as him, she was probably stronger, as he had never really done much physical labor. She might be a lot smarter, too. That last one hurt his pride. He had fell for the doggerel handed out at the meetings of the E.C.S. without question. He hadn't even considered the fact that mining, with absolutely no regulations, had been going on in the State for about a hundred years. Now, when the Miners were trying to make the water cleaner and reclaim the land previously mined, groups like his were trying to shut them down permanently. He had finally read some of the regulations Miners were expected to follow and could see where a lot of the problems arose.

The main problem was the classification of almost all of the rivers and streams in the entire State being classified as drinking water. Just because the Federal government was too lazy at the time to label each one separately, and lumped them all into one classification telling people it would be a simple matter to reclassify them individually, later. Most of the streams were so muddy and turbid that a person could practically chew the water. The clear water streams were rich in "Beaver Fever" or Giardiasis.

Anyone fool enough to drink from them without treating the water took a chance on a fate worse than Montezuma's Revenge. Now when anyone applied to reclassify a stream, the application was either not accepted or held a while then denied.

As far as his research had gone into the matter, it appeared maybe 3 streams had been reclassified since 1971. Family mining added no chemicals to the water, was more like accelerated erosion than pollution and affected only a few streams in the whole State. He was beginning to wonder what the big flap was all about. It rather seemed like overkill. At this rate, he was going to have to look for another line of employment.

Chapter 10

College had not prepared him for the realities of working in the field. He had majored in Environmental Sciences. Put into practice as applied to mining in Alaska, the classes offered no help. If he had gone to work in the Lower 48 States, with chemical pollution problems, he would have known what he was talking about. He did not care for the feeling this thought gave him. He thought he would like it even less as he researched more into the problem.

Now, since he was looking at studies other than the ones supplied by the E.C.S., there was a wealth of information available. It was probably a good thing he had a contract to continue his job until October 30th. He thought he would ask to terminate the contract before that date and figured it would please the Administrator of the E.S.C. He would probably help him pack his desk and show him the door.

Will was staying at the roadhouse in the little village about 30 miles away and the thoughts that filled his mind on the drive were not comforting, to say the least. He would stop back at the cabin and see if anyone had thought of anything they would like brought out from Fairbanks, next week.

Mike had been walking, when he stopped at Jo's, so walked back, thinking over the last few hours. Lorraine was certainly a pretty little thing, but he could not get Jo's kiss off his mind. The fact that Jo continued to mine and seemed set on staying here was in her favor, but he still thought she was working for the "Greenies".

Harlan had told him about the rag in her intake and also the fact that someone was still messing around her sluice box. She had to clean the upper riffles daily to ensure that she would get the fruits of her labor. Mike was sure that someone was snooping around their sluice boxes also. He was glad that there was usually someone in the trailer, most of the time, his Dad.

If he were honest with himself, Dad wasn't much good as a guard in the evenings. Since he and Mom had divorced, Dad didn't have to look for excuses to drink himself into a stupor almost every evening. It was only a wonder Mom hadn't left him years before she did. He would just have to start paying more attention, himself. It wouldn't do to lose their pay out of the box. That represented their year's earnings. Maybe he would also start dropping by and getting better acquainted with the girls. Tonight had been fun.

The women rehashed the evening as they prepared for bed. All in all, they thought it a great deal of fun and was looking forward to doing it again next week.

Maybe they would plan a special meal for everyone. Jo thought they could figure out something easy, yet tasty. Harlan and Thad had shown her some of the edible mushrooms and she had been gathering them after each little rain shower. She and Lorraine would have to do a lot of planning and make the party something to remember.

The women's' routine didn't vary much during the next week. They were starting to can some of the garden produce as it ripened. It seemed to grow fast enough to watch the progress every day. The wild raspberries were ripening as fast as the blueberries, so they spent a good portion of each day picking, cleaning and preserving the berries. The weather was nearly perfect for the garden and wild berries.

So even if there wasn't much water for mining, she wouldn't starve if she put enough foods up for the long winter. She would have to set enough money back to replenish the fuel she had used this season, but that wouldn't take too much as she hadn't operated to capacity. She thought she probably had enough, now, for fuel and to buy the necessities for the cabin.

She would have to go to Fairbanks in late August or September to get her supplies and winter gear. Well, guess her subconscious had made up her mind for her to spend the winter out here. Now that that was settled, she would really have to sit down and make some lists. Everything she would like to have, and everything she actually needed. If she had any money left after the really need list was taken care of, she would start on the like list.

In the evenings, Jo and Lorraine started making lists. Lists of what they each thought would be needed to spend the winter. Lorraine said she thought Jo should give a lot of thought to adding another gas light or two, to the cabin interior. All those hours of darkness might get on a person's nerves in a little cabin with only 3 small windows.

Grampa had one light by the table and one by the stove and that was it. Jo decided Lorraine was probably right. Lorraine had asked Will to look into the cost of going to the University of Alaska at Fairbanks, when he stopped on his way back out.

He had picked up everyone's mail at the little Post Office and the women made mail delivery to all the places they knew, then left the rest with Harlan. Will was surprised at Lorraine's request, but pleased and promised to look into it. Lorraine whispered something to him as he was leaving and he smiled and nodded. Jo didn't give it any thought. She was just glad that they seemed to be getting along.

The women decided to fix a large pot of spaghetti with fresh baked garlic bread and salad. They had found some nice large mushrooms to add to the canned meat sauce. Fresh onions and celery from the garden helped the sauce along, also. While they worked on the bread dough, Jo decided they might as well make a large batch so there would be enough for some cinnamon rolls. She hadn't made any since the first batch, when she first met Will. Surely this time would go better.

Harlan and Thad showed up early to "help out" and kept them laughing with stories and jokes. The afternoon passed quickly and their preparations were almost complete when Will and Mike arrived. Mike was walking along the road and Will offered him a ride. They were both a bit surprised when he accepted. They still acted like they would almost as soon hit each other as not, but managed to keep it under control. As the evening progressed they seemed to forget their mutual animosity and entered into the fun. The meal was a great success and so were the cinnamon rolls.

Will said he had something in the truck for the girls and went back out to get it. Lorraine could hardly contain her smile. Will came back in with a large box that gave off funny little noises. He had a sheepish look on his face as he set the box on the floor.

Nestled in a large fluffy blanket was a darling black and white malamute puppy and two small kittens. One kitten was fluffy and mostly white, with black feet and mustache. The other was marked more like a Siamese only with a lot of white included.

Jo immediately fell in love. The three baby animals were so adorable and they were piled in a heap, sleepy eyed and complaining about being disturbed. Will had placed a small clock in the box and the ticking seemed to make the babies think their mother's heartbeat was near and gave them a feeling of security. They immediately went back to sleep. Will brought in a large bag of food for the puppy, then another for the kittens and a bucket of litter.

Then he explained how he had gotten them. Lorraine mentioned Jo needed a dog or a cat. He saw the puppy in a litter some kids were giving away at a supermarket and the kittens would be going to the animal shelter. If Jo didn't want them, he would try to find homes for them, but she had first pick. They were so darling, she couldn't just take one of them. So she was now the proud owner of not just one but three animals. In days to come she would be more inclined to think the small animals now owned her, for they required much care as young as they were.

The next day, Mike drove over in an ancient old truck, with a dog house on the back. He made it that morning, out of small logs so it looked like a miniature of the big cabin. He seemed embarrassed now, that he had done it and brought it over. Jo and Lorraine thought it was wonderful and made much over him, with coffee and cinnamon rolls. He wondered why he had been staying away. The companionship was wonderful, the food was delicious and he hadn't felt so good in a long time. But he had better get back to work, his Dad was giving him a bad enough time about building the little house for "that woman's" dog. The fact that Jo had stood up to him over the matter of her dozer still rankled the man. Even though he had been in the wrong, he managed to make it all her fault.

The women decided to go for the mail the next

day. So they went around to everyone, picking up anything needing sent out. They decided to take the babies with them, as they would be gone such a long time. So when they set off, the box was in the middle of the front seat, the little ones in residence, with a girl on each side. The trip was uneventful and Jo had a lot of mail waiting for her. Several from her family and one from Steve Mathews, Grampa's attorney.

They decided to splurge and have lunch at the roadhouse and read the letters then. They picked up a couple of T-shirts at the Trading Post that had Alaskan sayings on them.

While waiting for their order, Jo was surprised to see Bill Humphries come in at the door. She turned her back and hoped he would ignore her. Now why was he still hanging around? Maybe she had better read her mail.

The letter from the attorney had good news and bad news. On further investigation, it appeared the Grampa's accident was man made. There was not enough evidence to point a finger at anyone, or even to re-open the initial investigation. For the time being, it would remain as accidental death. He advised Jo to be very careful and not to be alone any more than necessary. Jo filled Lorraine in on this and the possibility that there might be some future unknown danger. Also, the company that George Watson represented assured them that they would not pursue the purchase of Jo's clams.

Mr. Mathews had started investigating the reasons

for their interest and it seemed a possibility of some diamonds being found in the area. Probably industrial grade, but still of value. Lorraine poked Jo, whispering, "There's a very good looking fellow at the bar that keeps staring over here at your back. He's really gorgeous. Do you know him?"

"Yes, I'm afraid I do. That's my ex-fiance and in my opinion, he is a total jerk."

"Oh, but he's soooo good looking. Maybe he wants to make up with you, if he came all the way up here to be near you."

Their order came and as they started to eat, Bill came into the dining room. He had a drink in his hand, even though it was only noon. Jo had never seen him drink as much as she had seen in just the last two times she had seen him, here, in Alaska. To her, he acted like he had a guilty conscience about something and was trying to brave it out on alcohol. As he reached their table, she could tell this wasn't his first drink of the day, either. His face was flushed and his eyes were slightly puffy and red rimmed. He pulled out a chair and sat down with them.

"So, how's Miss High and Mighty today? Ready to discuss the sale of the property like you should be or still playing Lady Miner? I need that money and I need it soon, so you'd better hurry up and get this foolishness out of your system."

Jo was flabbergasted at his assumption that she would sell an to top it all off, give him the money. "Bill, I'm not going to sell, not now, nor in the foreseeable future. Even if I did sell, I would never give you the money. I don't see where you think you have the right to it, anyway. It would be my money, to do with as I see fit and I certainly don't think you are anywhere near the priority list. You're fast getting to be on the shit-list as far as I am concerned."

Lorraine giggled and Bill seemed to notice her for the first time. "Say, who do we have here? Aren't you the pretty little girl. What about dinner tonight. I have a cabin near here that I am renting. As soon as Jo realizes I'm doing this for her own good, she can go on home and we can have a little party."

How could he, Jo fumed. He must have been drinking a lot more than she first thought. He had never been so open in trying to pick up someone else. She sort of knew he was unfaithful to her even while they were planning to marry. But this was plain stupid.

Lorraine was speechless. She had thought Jo was exaggerating his faults but now she thought maybe Jo was being charitable. This guy was a real jerk. Had Jo really been going to marry him? What a lucky escape.

Bill spotted the letter from Steve Mathews and snatched it from under Jo's hand.

As he read it, his face darkened and he threw the paper back at her. "What the hell are you talking to some lawyer for? Why can't you just let me handle this and keep him out of it? I talked to him and he doesn't impress me at all. I think he is just a shyster.

I have a buyer and he's eager to settle this as soon as possible. I don't know how long I can keep him interested, if you don't hurry up and sign the papers."

"Bill, haven't you heard a word I've said? I'm not selling. Forget it and go home. This is my home now and I am staying. Get that through that thick skull of yours, once and for all."

"Oh come on. You're going to marry me and you know it. This little fling of independence is all well and good. But your family would like to have you near them. You know they could use the extra help. My place s needing a lot of work too and it's not getting any better, the longer you stay here. I've already borrowed the money needed to fix up the place, but I need the sale of this property to meet the note. The bank wouldn't lend it to me, so I went to some "friends" that loan short term. But they can be pretty nasty if it's not paid back on time."

"Then all in all, why aren't you back there, trying to get the money from your own place to pay them back? I'm not giving you a dime."

His face contorted in fury and he slapped her across the face as fast as his hand could move. Without thinking, she drew back and slugged him in the jaw. His face went slack and he slid to the floor. Jo's hand was swelling and she was afraid she might have broken a bone, but what about Bill? Was he okay? Lorraine calmly threw her glass of ice water in his face. He sputtered and groggily sat up. Things were certainly not going as planned. Jo was supposed to be so grateful that he still wanted to marry her, that she would give him anything. What on earth had hit his jaw? It felt twice it's normal size. Now who was this, hauling him up by the front of his shirt and dumping him out the door?

Mike had came in for a hamburger and was just in time to see Bill slap Jo and Jo deck Bill. The woman had a good swing, but she would have to learn not to hit bone that way. It was a good way to break something. Mike grabbed Bill by the shirt and dumped him out the door.

"Don't you ever lay a hand on either one of those women again. I'll look you up and really give you a working over if I hear about it. If she hadn't already prettied up one side of your face, I'd stomp you for hitting her. It would be a good idea to get out of here, before I decide to do it anyway, on general principle. Anyone that hits women deserves whatever he gets. Oh, you look uneven."

So saying, Mike punched him on the other side of his face to even him up and left him laying in a heap outside the door.

The cook brought a bowl of ice and Jo was soaking her hand in it. The fingers all worked okay so there was probably nothing broken. Mike and the cook both suggested that Jo go over to the health aide to make sure. Mike and Lorraine escorted Jo to the health aide's cabin. They joked and laughed about the way Bill looked as they trooped past him. He had crawled over under a tree and was sleeping off his mid morning drunk. His face was not going to be so pretty for a while. Maybe he would think twice before hitting someone again. If he even remembered what happened.

The health aide checked out Jo's hand and suggested she aim for a more tender place to hit, next time. The health aide was inclined to gossip a bit and told them that Bill had been making a real pest of himself in the village. He was drinking heavily and bragging about making a bundle of money soon. No one paid much attention to him, but he had fast worn out his welcome. He was staying with a woman in her cabin near the river. If she found out about his trying to pick up Lorraine and still considered himself engaged to Jo, she would probably throw him out into the river. He had been making her a lot of promises.

Chapter 11

Lorraine asked if she could practice her driving on the way back to the cabin. She hadn't had a chance to drive much but did have a beginners permit. Jo decided her hand could use the rest, so Lorraine was elated to find herself perched behind the wheel of the big old pickup. She could barely see over the dash, so the blanket was taken from the box of animals and made into a cushion under her. The seat was pulled forward as far as it would go and her feet just did reach the pedals. She had never driven a manual transmission before so they hopped their way out of town as she tried to find the gears and let the clutch out gently. It was with a great feeling of accomplishment that she pulled up in the front yard of the cabin and stalled the engine.

Thad was sitting on the bench, waiting for them and applauded her as she jumped down from the pickup. She curtsied elaborately in her blue jeans and handed him his mail. They sat in the cabin with a cool can of soda each and read their mail and visited. Lorraine told Thad all about Jo's meeting with Bill and the outcome. Thad cautioned Jo to be on the lookout for possibly more trouble from him.

Said it looked like Bill was in a spot and wouldn't take kindly to being thwarted by her refusal to go along with his plans. The girls promised to keep an eye out for him and stay out of his way, if possible.

The women spent the evening writing letters to their families and talking over the day's happenings. Jo's family still seemed to be of the opinion that Jo and Bill were just having a little lover's tiff and would soon return home and get married. Jo tried to think of something that would once and for all set them straight. Lorraine told her to tell them about the way Bill had been, today. If that didn't do it, nothing would. So Jo wrote them of the day's happenings. She hated to disillusion them about their neighbor, but she didn't want to marry him to please them, either. They wouldn't have to be the one living with him.

The women decided they wanted to pick real Alaskan names for the puppy and kittens so started going through some of the books, looking for suitable names. They finally settled on Sitka for the pup and Toolik and Atigun for the kittens. The kittens delighted in tumbling over the puppy and he would make mock rushes at them. He made small sounds but did not bark at all. The three babies soon tired themselves out playing and collapsed in a heap and went to sleep. The women were surprised to see it was after midnight, so went to bed.

Jo awoke to tiny fierce growlings and found the little ones all at the door with their fur fluffed out and ears back, growling in their tiny throats. Jo looked out the window and saw a large bear near the door. Jo poked Lorraine to wake her up and motioned toward the window with her finger to her lips. Lorraine came groggily over to the window and let out a squeal of fright as the bear swung his huge head and looked right at her. Jo turned the radio up loud and banged a kettle with a spoon The bear turned and ambled off into the brush. Lorraine was no longer groggy.

The women picked up their tiny defenders and soothed their fur and congratulated them for being such good watch puppy and kitties. The little ones snuggled next to them and were soon sound asleep. But Jo and Lorraine couldn't do the same.

"That was a huge bear and he didn't really seem afraid of us. He won't come back, will he?" Lorraine asked.

" I don't know, Grampa always said to never leave anything around that a bear might like the smell of. They will eat just about anything. That's why we burn all the cans and garbage before hauling it to the dump. It kills the odor of food. Maybe he was just curious. We will have to watch out for him and keep Sitka, Atigun and Toolik in the house. They would just be appetizers for something that big."

Neither woman felt much like sleeping, so they talked about their homes and growing up. Lorraine was the baby of the family and they never let her forget it, while Jo was the oldest and always expected to set a good example for the younger ones. It was interesting to talk about the different things expected of them and not being related, they could sometimes see how things were in their own homes, from the other's perspective.

When they finally gave up and got up, then went outside, they could see that the bear had snooped around the sheds and left scratch marks high on the wall of the tallest shed. The bear had not really bothered anything and they hoped it stayed that way. Jo wasn't too confident that the shotgun would even slow something that big, down, let alone kill it. She didn't want to kill the bear, especially this time of year. The fur would not be in good shape and the weather was too warm for keeping the meat.

Sitka, Atigun and Toolik followed close on their heels as they made their inspection. All three were very jumpy and growled at everything that moved, a squirrel, some leaves, a vole. They were very happy to get back to the cabin and didn't complain about being locked in for the morning. Lorraine wore Jo's pistol and Jo carried the shotgun as they left the cabin to work.

The bear didn't come around again, so the women were able to relax, until they mentioned it to Thad. He said bears usually had a circuit and would take from a week to 10 days to come around again. He may not come right up to the cabin, unless something interested him, but the fact that he had marked one shed showed that he considered it part of his property.

Mike had started coming over about every other evening and the women always tried to have some sort of sweet on hand. Harlan and Thad were regulars at these impromptu gatherings, too, and everyone enjoyed themselves very much. Usually the fellows would pick a container of berries for the women and then tease them about having to work for their treats.

The next time that Will came out, he arrived just as Jo had decided to make some taffy. Everyone had showed up and there would be plenty of hands to pull it properly. Will brought ice cream in his cooler, so everyone had ice cream and blueberry pie while the candy cooked.

Jo was confused about her feelings for Mike and Will. Both had kissed her and both seemed more like good buddies since then. Was there something wrong with the way she kissed? Neither one seemed to want any more from her than the good times they shared with the whole group. What was worse, she couldn't decide which one she liked the most. They were both nice fellows and she had definitely enjoyed their kisses. She was preoccupied with cooking the candy and didn't notice the way Mike and Will each watched her. Each immediately assumed the other had done something to upset Jo. So they spent the evening alternately watching Jo and glaring at each other.

The candy turned out well anyway. It was eaten almost as fast as they could safely do so without burning themselves. No one was sure if it would have hardened right or not, but no one cared. Lorraine got a kick out of watching her brother watch Jo. She looked at Harlan and Thad and they all winked at each other. Lorraine giggled and everyone wanted to know what was so funny. She pointed at Sitka, with a drop of candy stuck in the fur above his nose, trying to lick it off. Atigun and Toolik thought it was a new game and were trying to catch his tongue. Everyone started laughing and the kittens renewed their efforts. Sitka thought this was great and it developed into a small scale brawl. Soon they were in a heap of sleeping little bodies.

The rest of the evening was spent in quiet talk and everyone was in good spirits by the time they went home. There was getting to be an hour or two of dusk in the middle of the night now, so Will gave Mike a ride home.

As soon as they were down the road a ways, each started to speak, stopped, then started again. Finally Mike said "What have you done to upset Jo?"

"Me? I thought you did something. She don't even like me most of the time. I thought she was going to kill me, when I went to see her at the hotel in Fairbanks."

"Sure didn't look like it when I saw you two. You had your arms hanging all over each other."

So Will told Mike everything that happened up to the point of Mike's having seen them in the hall.

Mike was collapsed in laughter by the time Will was finished.

"Well, I'm glad someone thinks it's funny. I thought I was going to have to become a monk, in the very least, after that. Don't ever sneak up on her. She is lethal."

Mike told Will how he had thought he was hallucinating, after his first encounter with Jo. Then was stupid enough to do the same thing again. By the time Mike got out of Will's truck, at his trailer, they were on far better terms than they had ever thought possible. But neither one still had any idea what was bothering Jo. Maybe Lorraine could give them a clue.

Lorraine could have, but decided she wouldn't. It was kind of funny seeing her know-it-all brother with a problem. She would talk to Jo, though. She didn't want Jo to be hurt by the pigheadedness of the guys.

Lorraine had gone berry picking and Jo was canning some vegetable soup when she heard a vehicle pull up in the yard. She had just dried her hands and was reaching to open the door when a fellow pushed it open. Jo stood with her hand on the shotgun, leaned against the door jamb but out of the man's sight.

"Excuse me, but what do you think you are doing?" Jo asked.

"I just bought these claims and cabin and I'm giving you about 10 minutes to move out or I'm going to throw you out."

"May I see your papers and by what authority you propose to do this? I inherited this property from my grandfather and am the sole heir to it."

The man started to push Jo aside, but her hand had gripped the shotgun and she pulled it up between them. The man didn't see what she had in her hand at first and knocked her back onto the couch.

"Listen, you. I paid good money to Bill Humphries for this property. He said there was some stupid broad living here that would claim it was hers. He told me you would say anything to keep this ground."

Jo brought the gun up as he advanced toward her. She didn't now what to do, he was ignoring the gun and she didn't want to shoot him. But as he advanced, he raised his fist as though to strike her so she pulled the hammer back on the gun. The loud click seemed to finally penetrate his thick skull and he stopped. Jo could smell the liquor on his breath and fear knotted her stomach. No telling how much the man had drank or what he would do.

"I would suggest that you drive back to Fairbanks and check up on the ownership of this property. Bill Humphries has never owned it in the first place, so I am not sure how he can sell it to you. Contact Steve Mathews in Fairbanks and he will tell you about this property. He was my grandfather's attorney and has been handling things for me."

The man seemed hypnotized by the shotgun barrel. "Now see here, we can work something out. Bill said this was good property and I paid just about every dime I could raise to buy it. What am I supposed to do now?"

Hadn't the man been listening? "Look, I don't see what I am supposed to do for you. But I would suggest that you try to get your money back out of Bill. He's probably on his way to the Lower 48 right now. But if you hurry, you may be able to stop him before he gets out of Fairbanks."

The man hurried out the door and Jo collapsed on the couch. Good heavens, what would Bill not stoop to, to get the money for his ranch? The man must be a bit mentally deranged. How could she possibly stop such a thing happening in the future? She didn't want to always have to be looking over her shoulder, afraid someone was going to try to evict her from her own property.

Lorraine returned a short time later and the two women discussed the problem. They decided to talk it over with Harlan and Thad and then would probably go to the village and call Steve Mathews. He might know what they could do.

After talking it over a bit more, they decided just to start with calling Mr. Mathews. They would go, first thing in the morning. He could alert the proper authorities about Bill Humphries' activities.

Every time Lorraine tried to talk to Jo about the guys, Jo said she didn't know what Lorraine was thinking about, but she was wrong and there was nothing to discuss. Lorraine tried again as they were preparing for bed. Jo still thought it was a figment of Lorraine's imagination. Will and Mike were both interested in her? Impossible. It would be rather nice to have someone interested in her for herself though, instead of for what she could do for them.

Jo's dreams that night, were populated by

handsome men, all wanting to marry her. In the background of her dreams lurked a shadowy figure, not amongst the ones vying for her attention, that she somehow knew was the one she should marry. What a confusing dream. She didn't think she would ever have to worry about it coming true. The only person that actually wanted to marry her was Bill and she would rather go through life by herself than to marry him.

As the women were having breakfast, Thad drove up in his old Cadillac. He said he just happened to be going to the village that morning and would the ladies like to ride with him? Harlan was busy, but said he would stop over and check on things if the ladies wanted to go. Perfect, they would go.

Chapter 12

After calling Mr. Mathews' office and learning that he wouldn't be in for another hour, the women each called their families. Lorraine was surprised to hear that her mother was starting to get out and see people again. In fact, her mother sounded almost like she used to do. Lorraine was amazed and happy for her.

Jo's family was upset because of Bill Humphries. Bill arrived late a few nights ago, banging on their door. He asked, then demanded that they loan him money to save his ranch. When refused, he stormed out and they had not seen him since. There was a sign on the property the next day, listing it for sale. Then another fellow showed up, looking for Bill. He said Bill sold him someone else's property in Alaska and he was going to get his money back, one way or another. Whatever had she done to Bill? He was always such a nice young man. There was even a girl in town saying she was going to have Bill's baby. It was all so very confusing. They just wished Jo had married Bill, settled down next door and everything would have been so nice.

Jo didn't quite know what to think of this

convoluted line of thinking. When she hung up, she still didn't know whether her family really expected her to take the blame for all of Bill's faults and problems or if they were just disappointed that she would probably be living so far from them in the future. She hoped it was the latter.

Mr. Mathews was very reassuring, when she finally talked to him, later. He would send her a letter with the results of his investigations, so far, on what they had discussed at their meeting. He was planning on being in the area in a couple of weeks and she invited him to stop in and see them.

Thad insisted that they all needed lunch at the roadhouse before making the 30 mile drive back to the cabin. As they walked in to the roadhouse, Thad let out a whoop and dashed over to a table in the corner. He grabbed the lady sitting there and they hugged each other and he almost collapsed into the chair she was sitting on. Thad motioned the young women over and introduced them to a hefty little white haired lady that was looking them over with laughter in her eyes.

"Girls, I want you to meet the only true love of my life, Fanny Mae. Fanny, this is Jo Atkins, Jeremy's granddaughter and this is Lorraine Turner, a friend of Jo's. They're living in Jeremy's place, well, it's Jo's place now. How long you been back in town, Darlin'? Why haven't you been out to see me? Won't Harlan have a fit when he finds out you're here. Ha, that'll teach him to stay home."

Fanny Mae was about 5 feet tall and just about as

wide. She had a halo of snow white hair and snappy black eyes that looked like a young girl's. She had been a beauty when young and still had a lovely face.

Her hands were pudgy and she had gold nugget rings on almost every finger. She was dressed in an outfit that looked vaguely in style, 50 years ago. But she did it in style and it suited her. She invited them to sit at her table and proceeded to entertain them in high style for the next couple of hours. Thad checked his watch, then looked again. "I hate to say this, girls, but I have to be getting back. Harlan will be worrying if we don't show up pretty soon. You coming out with us, Fanny?"

Fanny agreed, if they could stop by her cabin so she could pick up a few things to take with her.

The trip back to the cabin seemed to only take a few minutes. No one even noticed the dirt road and all the bumps. Harlan was waiting for them at Jo's cabin when they pulled in. As soon as he spotted Fanny, he trotted over, swung the car door open and pulled her out of the car.

He wrapped his arms around her as far as he could reach and hugged her. Thad yelled out that since he saw her first, today, he had dibs. Everyone went in to the cabin, laughing and joking. They had cool drinks and some pie. Jo thanked Harlan for watching out for the animals and Thad for the ride to the village. He hadn't gotten anything for himself, that she could see, he just made the excuse to go, to help her. Of course, if he hadn't gone, he wouldn't know Fanny was back yet, either, but still, it was sweet of him.

After Harlan, Thad and Fanny left, the women went up to make their daily "splash". the weather remained warm an mostly dry so the tiny creek was almost dry. There was only enough water to wash gravel a few minutes each day and they didn't want to miss a day. Jo's bottle graduated to a larger size and was filling up steadily. She would have enough gold at the end of the summer to buy her winter supplies and next summer's fuel. She felt pretty good about that. She still hadn't needed to touch the nest egg in the bank in Fairbanks.

Sitka, Atigun and Toolik were growing fast. Sitka was fairly well housebroke now so that was a real help. He was so fuzzy he looked like a giant fuzz ball rolling around the cabin floor with the kittens. All three chased his tail, sometimes getting very rowdy.

The women had seen tracks of bears near the cabin, but so far, none bothered them. The garden was producing full production and they were working at preserving the vegetables and also picking more berries. The cellar under the cabin was getting well filled with jars of food. There were bins to store potatoes, turnips and carrots and the women cleaned them out very well before time to refill them. It would be about a month before they had to dig the potatoes, but it would be ready.

Several times, Inspectors from both State and Federal Agencies had been in the area, inspecting the mining sites. The state agents would tell the

Miner if he was non-compliant so he could try to meet the standards or shut down. The Federal agents never commented, one way or the other. They would surprise the Miner with a press release to the news that they were bringing charges against certain Miners, during the following winter. Many Miners in the past had first found out that they were under arrest by reading it in the newspaper or hearing it on the radio or TV.

Since Jo was not moving much dirt per day, she was considered a recreational Miner and the Inspectors had not bothered her. She was still expected to keep the water as clear as drinking water, but other than that, she would have no problem.

The women started cutting one load of firewood a day and hauling it back to the cabin after making their daily "splash". The wood pile in the shed was steadily getting bigger and Jo hoped she would be able to cut enough for the entire winter. She had finally decided yes, she was spending the winter out here in her own cabin and thought she would do okay. Most of the people in the area either moved to Fairbanks or the village for the winter although several lived out of State.

August, which was always so hot back at the ranch, saw the start of rain almost every day. One evening on the way back to the cabin from the outhouse, Jo saw her first Northern Lights. The sight was awe inspiring. Never had she imagined the beauty and movement of the lights. The closest she could come to describing them was a chiffon curtain billowing gently in a breeze. Sometimes moving in slow stately motion, then whipping around and shooting steaks of color across the sky. The bottom of the curtain was bright pink, shading into yellow and green as it reached higher into the sky. Jo yelled at Lorraine to come outside and they both stood in awe, watching this magnificent show of lights. The still photos that looked so lovely in the stores in Fairbanks didn't even begin to capture the moving living lights. No wonder so much myth and fables had grown up over the centuries about the lights.

The letter from the attorney was reassuring, but hadn't really solved anything. George Watson had been reprimanded by his company for his tactics in trying to scare her into selling her property. They were sending Mr. Mathews a copy of their preliminary geological report on her claims as a conciliatory measure. Steve Mathews was due, Saturday, at the cabin. Jo and Lorraine invited everyone in the area over for a party.

Will was due to come out from Fairbanks, also, and was bringing some bags of ice for cold drinks. Most of the overflow ice on all of the creeks had finally melted. Any that was left was so dirty no one wanted to use it. Will was bringing some other goodies also. Lorraine hoped he would bring some nice steaks. She was getting tired of canned or dried meat.

Chapter 13

Lorraine was learning to cook and bake quite well during her stay with Jo and also grown up quite a bit. She decided to move back to Fairbanks and enroll at the University. She would present Will with a plan to do his housework and cooking in exchange for room and board and see what kind of reaction she got from him. She was 18 now and trying to act in a responsible manner, if he would give her the chance.

The morning of the party was dull and rainy so the women decided to do the baking early. The extra heat in the cabin would be welcome. Fanny came by and added a rowdy sense of humor to the proceedings. She came to Alaska when she was 16 and worked in the dancehalls. She mined more gold at night than the men ever did during the day, she told the women. When she finally retired, she owned several claims and leased them to a large company that supplied her with a tidy retirement. She had enjoyed her life and still did.

Thad and Harlan came by and the rest of the day was spent in reminiscence. The three of them each trying to outdo the other in outrageous stories. Steve Mathews arrived during one of the more implausible stories and added the final chapter to it. Jo and Lorraine were very surprised to learn that it was, indeed, true.

Mr. Mathews insisted they call him Steve and he seemed to shed the roll of attorney before their eyes. He had just returned from a case in Washington, D.C. and was glad to be back in Alaska. He flirted with Fanny and Thad indignantly told him to forget it, she was spoken for. Fanny laughed and said she had been spoke at, to and about, but didn't remember being spoken for. Anyway, she liked younger men. Thad pretended to be outraged by this, so Fanny proceeded to cuddle up to him and batted her eyelashes at him and begged his forgiveness. Everyone enjoyed themselves very much and the party hadn't even started yet. Steve declared that if Fanny was off limits, he would just have to console himself with the other girls available and set out to flirt with Jo and Lorraine. Fanny told him he was just fickle, like most men. Then all three men denied being fickle, just misunderstood.

Will arrived and brought a bag of groceries. Steve went out to his car and brought in another bag of groceries, also, for an informal feast. Both men brought steaks so there were enough for the whole group present and a few more drop ins, if they showed up later. As the steaks broiled, the women fixed the salad and vegetables. There would be fresh hot biscuits and later, dessert. Will had ice cream in his cooler for the pies he knew the women would have.

Mike showed up just as the steaks were done, so joined them for dinner. Will and Mike didn't know what to make of Steve's flirtatious manner with Jo and Lorraine. Steve had beautiful silver hair, but his face was unlined and he was not old, by any stretch of the imagination. He was lean, tanned and very personable with an active mind and imagination. Will and Mike immediately decided they didn't like him, but couldn't stick to it. He was so charming and genuinely likeable that they found themselves liking him in spite of themselves.

Jo was confused by the whole thing. She found that she was very much attracted to Steve, even though he was only kidding around. When he put his arm around her and smoothed her hair back from her flushed face after she removed a pan from the oven, a spark seemed to pass between them. She knew he felt it too, by the look that suddenly flashed in his eyes. He had not touched her since and confined his flirting to Lorraine. Lorraine joined in with outrageous behavior and added flirting with Mike. Mike was uncomfortable at first, then joined the spirit of the game.

After dinner, the men told the women to sit and relax, they would do the dishes. Steve washed, Will and Mike dried and Thad and Harlan decided where to put everything. It would be a wonder if Jo could ever find half the stuff, tomorrow.

Other neighbors started showing up soon after the dishes were finished and soon the cabin was filled with people and laughter. One couple brought guitars and Harlan had his harmonica and soon music filled the cabin. The platters of snack food disappeared like magic and Jo was glad she had baked twice as much as she thought she would need. Several people brought bottles that were passed around from glass to glass but no one appeared to drink too much.

Mike said his father wouldn't be there, so it was a surprise to everyone when he showed up late in the evening. He had not been drinking, which surprised Mike most of all. He seemed rather subdued but soon was having a good time.

As the party broke up, he thanked Jo for an enjoyable evening and gruffly apologized for his previous behavior. He even offered payment for the use of her dozer for the time he had used it. Jo was flabbergasted but told him thanks, that is what neighbors are for.

Jo and Lorraine fixed up one of the small sheds as a little bunkhouse, behind the cabin. Steve and Will would be staying there for the night. Soon everyone was gone that was leaving so Jo, Lorraine, Will and Steve sat around the table and rehashed the evening.

Sitka, Atigun and Toolik came out from under the bed and joined everyone for a midnight snack. The general opinion was that everyone had enjoyed the evening very much. The Aurora was putting on a lovely display as Steve and Will left the cabin for their little bunkhouse. The women stepped out to enjoy the lights with the men, The Aurora formed a circle, dancing directly over their heads, then shot out spokes in all directions from the circle. It looked very similar to a large wagon wheel, spinning on fire in the sky. Tonight, the color was predominately fluorescent pink with tints of green on the upper edges and very beautiful. As the lights faded out, Will found his voice, "I have never seen anything like that in my entire life. Sure makes a person feel rather insignificant, doesn't it?"

"This was your first sight of the lights? Yes, they are magnificent." Jo said. "I think they are a special treat, every time I see them."

"So do I and I have lived up here all my life. I never tire of watching them." said Steve.

As Steve and Lorraine walked farther toward the bunkhouse, Will turned to Jo. She was closer than he expected and he bumped into her. He put out his hands to steady her and it seemed the most natural thing in the world to just keep putting his arms on around her and pulling her closer still. His lips seemed to have a mind of their own and he kissed her, softly at first, then with growing hunger. The spell of the lights seemed to still hold her and she mindlessly kissed him back.

Lorraine came around the corner, still looking for the lights to return and ran head-on into them. "Oh, here you are, Will., Steve has the light lit in the bunkhouse and is taking the bottom bunk. There's a small stove, if you need some heat." Her eyes dancing, Lorraine went on into the cabin.

Will went on to the bunkhouse and Jo came back into the cabin. Whatever was wrong with her, Will was not the type of fellow she was attracted to, so why was her head spinning and a wanting inside her that she had never experienced before from someone's kiss? Lorraine chose this moment to ask Jo how she liked Will. Jo mumbled something to the affect that he was okay and went to bed.

Her dreams were even more jumbled than usual and she awoke feeling like yesterdays' mush. Lorraine was up and fixing breakfast, singing a little song as she worked. It was disgusting for someone to be that cheerful when she felt so cold, lumpy and unlovable. Lorraine took one look at her, felt her forehead, decided she was coming down with a cold, possibly terminal, and sent her back to bed. Will and Steve came over and everyone commiserated with the bad luck of feeling so rotten on such a nice day. Sitka, Atigun and Toolik all climbed up on the bed and cuddled close to her, offering their own sympathy.

It was hard to remain grumpy and out of sorts with so much care and really, she could have gotten up to eat breakfast. But no, Will had some cans of orange juice under the seat of his truck and Lorraine had fixed a lovely breakfast of waffles with blueberry sauce. Steve decided that she had to stuff a cold or was that starve a cold, anyway, she had to eat to keep up her strength. Will thought she was probably strong enough, but didn't say so.

Soon, everyone was perched about her bed, eating breakfast and making such a fuss that Jo decided she had to feel better, she couldn't survive too much more of this care.

So after all the breakfast was eaten, she asked everyone to go outside so she could get dressed. Steve and Will both leered at her, saying they preferred to keep her undressed and in bed, but relented as she started throwing everything handy in their direction. As she dressed, she was surprised to find that she was indeed feeling much better. Maybe one did stuff a cold.

The fellows pitched in and helped around the shop. Will did some welding in his summer job during college, so was able to show Jo some of the rudiments of working the welder in the shop. He and Steve looked over the old pump and declared it not quite the disaster it seemed. If bribed properly, they might consider starting to repair it. She noticed they neglected to say they would complete the repairs on it. Jo brought this to their attention and they waved it away as trifles, lady, trifles. By noon, both men were greasy and looking grim, when called for lunch. Lunch restored their good spirits and when Jo brought out one of Grampa's bottles of homemade wine, everything was much better. By the time everyone returned to work, the mood had returned to the light banter and joking of the morning.

"A fine Environmentalist you are, Will. Repairing the lady's pump so she can rape and ruin the land more efficiently," Steve teased.

Will mentioned that he was looking for another line of work, anyway, and maybe this way he could get a reference from Jo. Lorraine told him her plan of going back to school this winter and he thought it sounded great. In fact, he might be going back to school, too, to learn a new profession. He was amazed that his featherbrained sister had such a good idea and planned it all out. Maybe she wasn't such a featherbrain, after all. Lorraine enjoyed working with her brother all day. It was the first time she could remember that he hadn't treated her like some little pest, in the way all the time. She would have to go to Fairbanks next week to get signed up for school and to move her stuff back to Will's. He looked forward to having help around the apartment. Since Lorraine had left, the place should be condemned by the health department. He was sure there was something growing in the refrigerator and possibly in the corner in the bathroom. He didn't even want to look under the beds. He was sure something had growled at him the last time he dared look under there. He hadn't thought Lorraine did anything around the place, until she left and none of it got done for him. She was actually a very good housekeeper.

Jo heated large containers of water during the afternoon and as everyone was very greasy and wanted a shower, she had them pack the water out and dump it in the tank above the outdoor shower house. It wouldn't be a hot shower, but it wouldn't chill a person to the bone, either. As long as no one used too much water, there would be warm showers for everyone.

The suggestion was made to conserve water and shower together but Jo and Lorraine declined. If the fellows were so water saver minded, they were welcome to shower together, though. They didn't think that was funny and certainly not what they had in mind.

The girls showered first, then prepared dinner while the men showered. As everyone finished eating, Thad, Harlan and Fanny pulled up in the old Cadillac. They were going to the village and wanted to know if everyone would like to go with them for an evening at the roadhouse. Mike showed up just as they were preparing to leave and deciding there was always room for one more, he was invited, also.

It was a good thing Thad and Harlan were both slender, with Fanny in the front seat between them. The front seat was crowded, but the five in the back seat were more than a snug fit. But the old car had more room than most so it was not as bad as they thought it would be. Lorraine sat on Mike's lap and Jo was firmly packed between Will and Steve. Steve laughed and said he hadn't done anything like this since he was about 18. It really brought back memories, whereupon he proceeded to kiss Jo. Jo was so startled that she didn't respond, one way or another. The kiss had been so brief it might not have happened, except the tingle of her lips and the look in Will's eyes. Steve was innocently looking out the window and whistled a little tune. Lorraine and Mike were talking and missed it, entirely. Will didn't know what to think and neither did Jo. Was she really reacting like this to just a harmless little kiss? Bill always hinted that she must be frigid and she had believed him. She never felt anything, one way or the other about his kisses. Now, she had been kissed by Mike, Will and Steve and every one of them made her long for more than just kisses. She squirmed uncomfortably in the seat, her thoughts and feelings very mixed. Even when Bill managed to convince her to spend the night with him, once in a while, she never felt any excitement when they made love. Now she seemed to be a mass of feelings and yearnings and three different men had each aroused these feelings in her. Maybe she was a late bloomer.

At the advanced age of 23 she should have experienced these feelings if she was ever going to, shouldn't she? She genuinely liked all three of the fellows and she couldn't recall ever really liking Bill. Thinking she loved him, she had not been blind to his lack of thoughtfulness to others. How had she ever managed to get engaged to him, anyway? She couldn't recall his ever actually asking her to marry him. It just sort of drifted into being, with everyone assuming they would marry. Thank goodness she wasn't going to actually go through with it. Maybe she was just starting to feel some good healthy lust. Deciding this, she smiled and enjoyed the rest of the ride to the village.

Someone brought a guitar to the roadhouse and a couple were singing. A space was cleared and a few couples were dancing. Mike swung Lorraine onto the floor and Will asked Jo to dance. Thad and Fanny were dancing, so Harlan and Steve pushed a couple of tables together for the group to come back to. They ordered some drinks and as the dancers came back to the tables, Steve asked Jo to dance. She accepted and the guitar played a slow dance. Jo fit perfectly into Steve's arms and once again that spark seemed to pass between them. Her blood felt like it was melting her body to his, her head felt like it was lightly spinning and she decided to relax and let nature take it's course. They danced like they had been dancing together all their lives and she was breathless although the dance was slow, at the end of it. Steve looked a little stunned also. As they sat at the table, his finger lightly stroked the back of her neck, leaving little trails of tingly fire in their wake. Every nerve ending in her body seemed alive and begging to be touched. Yes, this must be an attack of lust, alright. She had never felt anything like it in her life.

Will couldn't stand it. He had to get her away from Steve, even if she wasn't his type. Just what was her attraction, anyway? He always liked delicate, fragile little things that looked at him like he was their whole world. Of course they usually bored him silly after a month or two. But they were so nice on his ego. Why couldn't he get Jo out of his mind? She had changed his whole outlook on life, from his vocation to thinking he wouldn't mind having her around the rest of his life Whoa. Whatever was he thinking? The rest of his life?

Was he crazy? No way, he wasn't the marrying kind. Marry? Now where did that stray thought come from? Maybe live together for a while, but marry? Never! Will abruptly asked Jo to dance with him. He seemed so distracted she wasn't sure what the problem was, but maybe he would talk to her about it.

As they danced, he still seemed distracted and looked at her with a strange light in his eyes when she asked what was wrong. He held her hand as they left the dance floor and went right past their table and out into the night.

"Jo, will you move in with me?"

No preliminary talking, just blurt it out, it sounded rather bald to his own ears as soon as he said it.

"No, I mean, would you consider staying with us in Fairbanks this winter? Please? Lorraine would like that very much and I would, too." Will blundered on. Why didn't his mouth say the suave debonair things his mind had thought out? He was really botching this up very well.

"I'm sorry Will, but I want to spend the winter out here. I would be pleased to stay with you and Lorraine when I come to town for supplies, though, if that is all right? I have enjoyed Lorraine's company while she has been here and would like to continue seeing both of you."

Did he really mean it when he asked her to move in with him? As in, live with him? Or had he just blundered in the way he asked her to stay with him and Lorraine? She didn't want to presume too much. She turned to go back inside, Will miserably walking beside her.

Well, he had certainly blown that. Now she thought he was just asking to be kind, because of his sister.

They stayed a couple more hours, then decided to drive back to the cabins. Lorraine promptly fell asleep as they started back and later, Will was disgusted to find that he had, too. Steve cradled Jo up next to him and gently rubbed his thumb under her ear and jaw line. He found sensitive, tender spots that were building an inferno in her blood without even seeming to be aware of what he was doing. Jo didn't now whether to pull away or let his fingers work their magic. It felt so good, she decided to relax and just enjoy the sensations he was raising throughout her by just rubbing her earlobe.

Did every nerve in her body start from there? She could well believe it. She thought the books were exaggerating when describing how good it could feel. Now she thought maybe they were underestimating. Gently Steve tipped her head back and kissed a trail of fire from her ear toward her mouth. He delicately nibbled his way along and she thought she would die of longing before he actually reached her mouth. By the time he actually kissed her mouth, she felt as though they were drowning in a whirlpool of sensation. His other hand was moving in lazy circles along her ribcage and her breathing was having some sort of difficulty. This man definitely knew what he was doing, and he was doing it very well, indeed. So Bill thought she was frigid did he? Well, Bill was a bumbling idiot, for all of his experience. Bill had been intent on his own pleasure, this man seemed only to want to give her pleasure. He was definitely succeeding. She was afraid she would make some sound and everyone in the car would know what was happening in this dark corner of the car. Mike, Lorraine and Will were all asleep and it looked like Harlan and Fanny were, too. Thad was intent on his driving, humming a little tune as he kept his eyes on the road. Now that it was getting dark at night, he had to watch for large animals more carefully. Steve seemed to know what was bothering her and snuggled her back into his arms. He reassured her that nothing was going to happen and kissed her cheek. That's what she was afraid of, that nothing was going to happen. But how could she tell him that. He would think she was crazy. Maybe she was. But with Lorraine staying with her in the cabin and Will staying with him in the bunkhouse, she didn't see how they were going to manage anything but what had already happened. Steve continued to make his gentle assault on her senses and she did not resist, at all. In fact, she joined in as much as she could.

Finally he groaned and turned away from her a bit, "Honey, I'm sorry, but if we don't stop now, I'm going to embarrass us both."

Jo knew they were both in quite a state, but it had felt so darned good. She had never felt anything like this in her life. She would always remember this night with fond thoughts.

Thad pulled the car up in front of Mike's trailer and Mike sleepily wished them all a good night. The ride to Jo's cabin took only minutes and now Loraine and Will were both awake. Jo was glad for the darkness and the few minutes to compose herself before they reached her cabin. She thought she had succeeded quite well. Steve and Will went back to the little bunkhouse and Lorraine followed Jo into the cabin. As they prepared for bed, Lorraine started gently teasing her about teenagers necking in the backseat of cars and Jo started wondering just how sound asleep Lorraine had been. But when she looked in the mirror, she saw what Lorraine was teasing her about. Her mouth had a well kissed look about it and her eyes looked half drugged with longing. She was brushing out her hair when there was a light tapping at the door. She pulled her robe around herself and went to see who was at the door. Steve was standing there when she opened the door and his breath caught in his throat at the sight of her. Her hair was a shimmering curtain about her and the evidence of his kisses was plain to his eyes. He wanted nothing more at that moment than to continue where they had left off. He couldn't remember ever feeling this way about anyone before in his life.

"I just wanted to let you know I have to go back to Fairbanks early in the morning. I will be back out, this coming weekend, if that is alright with you."

He had to leave? In the morning? But he would

be back.

"Okay, come over as soon as you get up and we will have breakfast ready before you go. Of course you are welcome to come back next weekend. You are welcome any time, Steve. I have enjoyed having you here, very much."

What an understatement. Enjoyed him very much indeed, she would have really enjoyed him, given half a chance. She supposed she should be shocked at the way she was feeling and behaving, but somehow it seemed so right, at the time.

He had to force himself to turn around and walk back to the bunkhouse. Now why on earth had he gone down just to tell her that? He knew that Lorraine was there and that there was no possibility of saying or doing anything more than what he had just said.

He could have waited until morning to tell her he had to leave, but he just had to see her one more time before he went to bed. He had never seen her hair loose before. It was beautiful and added a new dimension to his dreams that night, which were jumbled enough. He was suffering from extreme frustration and hadn't acted like this since he was a kid. Will had his own private demons to contend with in the night and neither man got a very restful night's sleep. Neither did Jo. Lorraine was probably the only one that enjoyed a full night's sleep, uninterrupted by mentally kicking themselves for the way they were acting.

Jo felt surprisingly good in the morning for having

spent such a restless night. She had learned she was definitely capable of sensual feelings and of being aroused. That was something, anyway. She fixed a good breakfast and banged a spoon on a kettle to rouse the men. Steve whispered that she didn't need to arouse him and she blushed as she handed him his breakfast.

Will had to drive to the village again for some business and Lorraine invited herself to go with him. She winked at Jo as they left. Steve was surprised to find himself suddenly alone with Jo. They both felt a little awkward in the light of day, but it soon disappeared. Steve helped her with the breakfast dishes and as their fingers touched over the dishes, slowly the magic started building between them again.

Gently Steve kissed the back of her neck as he reached across for a dish, then his fingers were undoing the fastenings on her braid and her hair was floating free around her. He kissed her mouth then and that was the end of doing dishes for quite a while.

He undressed her as though he were unwrapping something very precious to him. His eyes drank in her body as he uncovered every square inch of it, his lips left trails of fire and his fingers seemed to be everywhere at once. She unbuttoned his shirt and trailed kisses across his chest. His body reacted the same as her own and surprised her. She hadn't known that. She had always been a bit ashamed of her body. It was not the fashionable size and shape, but he left no doubt about how much he desired her and that he thought she was beautiful. Just when she thought she could not stand any more sensation, she discovered that she could, and did. This was incredible, that the human body could feel so enraptured.

Afterwards, he held her close to him and stroked her body and face as he gazed at her. He was so thoughtful and considerate, that she didn't know what to think. Bill always jumped right up immediately and showered as though he couldn't stand the feel of her on his skin. Steve wanted to savor the moments and remained next to her, touching her and murmuring sweet words of praise. He pulled her hair over the both of them, like a cloak and held her close. She felt cherished and special, in his arms. Yes, there was a lot to be said for lust. This was marvelous.

Quite a while later, he reluctantly told her that he really did have to be back in Fairbanks that afternoon. But he would be back as soon as he could. She smiled and kissed him goodbye. Even if she never saw him again, he had given her something precious to remember.

The next week passed swiftly and Lorraine packed all of her belongings. She was excited about going back to school and had all kinds of plans for what she and Jo would do, when Jo came to Fairbanks. Mike came over several times and seemed to be forming a real attachment for Lorraine. Lorraine and Mike both wanted her to finish her schooling and Jo could only think that they were showing a lot of maturity in their decision.

Mike lived in Fairbanks during the winter, so they could continue seeing each other. Mike was at least a foot taller than Lorraine, but they were a very sensible young couple and Jo thought they would make a nice family, someday.

Chapter 14

Friday evening as Jo was taking a canner of vegetables off the stove, she heard an airplane buzz the cabin. She went outside and the plane circled again close over the cabin. She waved and the plane waggled it's wings and headed toward the landing strip.

She started the old pickup and went down to see what this was all about. As she pulled up near the plane, she was surprised to see Steve tying the plane to a large block of concrete.

"See? I said I would be back out as soon as possible. I brought dinner in the box, there, in the plane."

Tantalizing odors arose from the box, but first he hugged and kissed her soundly. They put the box and some other items he had brought into the pickup and she drove slowly up to the cabin. He insisted on kissing her several times on the way which didn't help her driving any. They were both as breathless, when they arrived, as though they had run the entire way. Lorraine insisted on unpacking the box of food immediately. She said her stomach couldn't stand the suspense. There were BBQ'd ribs, chicken, corn on the cob, potato salad and bean salad. Harlan came by just as they were setting the food on the table. He said he could smell the ribs when the plane went over. His nose just naturally led him right to them and of course the rest of his body had to follow.

After they ate, Mike came over in his pickup and he and Lorraine went to the village for the evening. Harlan left soon after and Steve and Jo sat looking at each other. She thought she should feel uncomfortable or nervous, but it seemed so natural when he reached his hand to her, that she automatically followed him to the bed.

She thought that the last time had been the best possible, but she found that it just seemed to get better and better, every time they made love. This could become habit forming.

When Lorraine and Mike returned, Jo and Steve were sitting on the couch, reading, with the radio on. Jo's hair was spread about her like a mantle and it looked so lovely, Lorraine told her she should leave it like that all the time. Jo laughed and told her to think about it, What would it look like while she was working, if it was flying loose. Lorraine admitted it probably wasn't too practical.

Mike left and Steve went out to the bunkhouse. Jo and Lorraine prepared for bed.

"Did you have a good evening?" Lorraine asked.

"Yes, very nice and you?"

"Oh, we danced a bit and talked about everything under the sun. Mike is such a nice guy, I really think that I am falling in love with him. He doesn't treat me like a child, but really seems to think of me as an equal. He said you had taught him a lot about women."

Jo didn't have a clue what Mike was talking about. It never dawned on her that maybe he thought she was a good example.

Steve started work on the pump as soon as he got up, the next morning. Jo found him hard at work when she went out to let him know breakfast was ready. He had picked up some parts in Fairbanks and brought them out with him. He thought the pump would be working in a couple of days.

Will arrived after lunch and everyone decided to take the rest of the day off. Steve's plane could carry 6 people, so they decided to fly over the Yukon River. There was a small village they could land at and buy some salmon.

The trip was exciting for Jo and Lorraine. They had never seen a river as large as the Yukon. It wandered back and forth across its large green valley. It is an extremely beautiful valley, the turbid river supported a large variety of fish, fowl and animal life. The little village was nestled in a bend of the river and they made a nice landing on the dirt strip.

Children and dogs curiously tagged along as they walked over to the little trading post. The fellow at the trading post directed them to a cabin where they could buy some nice fresh fish. The chubby lady that answered the door didn't seem at all surprised to find strangers at her door, wanting to buy fish.

She gave them some strips of smoked salmon, known as squaw candy, to chew on while she went down to the river bank. There was a large contraption tethered to the bank, that turned slowly in the water. As the paddles came up, once in a while a salmon would slide down the guide and into the waiting box. The lady swiftly reached down and grabbed a still wriggling salmon. She held it up for their approval and Steve nodded yes, she flipped it onto the bank, then reached for another. Steve nodded again and she brought both fish up to the cabin. She went into the cabin and returned with an odd shaped knife. The handle was in the center of a sickle shaped blade. This was an ulu, or woman's knife. She proceeded to clean the fish with swift economical movements. She joyfully haggled with Steve over the price while she cleaned the fish and was very pleased when he handed her the money.

She went into the cabin and returned with some more of the salmon strips, these were a gift. They thanked her for the fish and walked back to the plane. The children were sitting in a circle quite a ways from the plane, playing a story game. Jo gave the oldest one the two packs of gum she had in her jacket pocket, to divide up with the other children. They shyly thanked her, then ran.

The flight back to the dirt runway was smooth and they saw several moose from the air. As they crossed one high ridge, a large grizzly bear stood up on his hind feet and watched them. His fur looked like silk, in the breeze with his under fur and legs being a dark chocolate brown and the ends of the body fur almost platinum blond.

After they returned to Jo's cabin, they built up a large fire and let it burn down to coals, in the yard. Steve prepared one of the fish to roast over the coals on a plank. Lorraine drove up to Harlan's place, then over to Thad's, then on to Mike's to invite everyone over to Jo's for a fish bake. Mike's dad even came over and they had a lovely evening.

The aurora even put on a show for them as the evening advanced. The mosquitoes had almost disappeared but now there were black gnats, white socks and no-see-ums to contend with, Jo kept several mosquito coils burning around the yard and that helped. Of course everyone was liberally coated in the summertime perfume of Alaska, bug repellant. Everyone had their own favorite brand but all agreed, never use perfume or scented soaps in the summer. The bugs loved them.

Jo took one of the lit coils into the cabin to clear the biting flying creatures out before bedtime. Steve took one over to the bunkhouse, too. Then they sat in front of the glowing embers of the fire and watched the light show in the sky. The moon was coming up, full, and dimmed the lights considerably. It would not be long now before the first frost hit but tonight was beautiful.

Jo wondered how her Grampa had ever gotten Steve to represent him. Steve told her that his father was an attorney and had known her grandfather for years. When he needed an attorney, he had hired his friend, the senior Mr. Mathews. After Steve joined his father in practice, he met Jeremy Atkins and on the retirement of Steve's father, Steve continued handling Jeremy's legal work.

Will was very confused. Jo seemed different, somehow. She still treated everyone the same and acted the same, but there was something about her that made her even more desirable to him. He found that he couldn't take his eyes off her, all evening and Lorraine started teasing him unmercifully. Damn it all, she was not his type of woman. Why did she persist in haunting his dreams, even while he was still awake. He growled at his sister and went muttering off to bed.

Jo gave Lorraine several jars of their canned vegetables and berries to take home with her. She had worked hard and helped with never a complaint about the work. The bugs, the weather and the lack of indoor plumbing, yes, but not the work. Even then, it was usually mutual grumbling when they were both tired. Jo enjoyed Lorraine's' company and would miss her.

Lorraine's gear was packed into Will's truck and the goodbyes said. Thad and Harlan each gave her a gold nugget, to be made into a necklace by one of the jewelers in Fairbanks. Fanny recommended one to Lorraine that was reasonably priced and would do a good job. Mike told her he would be moving back to Fairbanks the first week of October and would like to see her then, if not sooner.

Steve had to be in Fairbanks early the next

morning, so rather than depend on the weather cooperating, he would have to leave this afternoon. Will offered a ride down to the airstrip when they left, so he accepted. He told Jo he would be back as soon as possible and would bring some supplies for her, whenever she needed them.

Chapter 15

After everyone had left, the cabin felt rather empty. Sitka, Toolik and Atigun all piled onto her when she sat on the couch, each trying to outdo the others for attention. Sitka was growing at a very good rate and would be large enough to skijor with, this winter. Jo thought she should probably start teaching him to have a harness on, now, while he was still small. So she spent the afternoon making an adjustable harness that would grow with him, for a while.

He didn't know quite what to think of this strange new contraption, but if Jo thought it was what he should wear, well, he would humor her. The kittens thought it was something new for their enjoyment. They proceeded to attack the straps with mock ferocity, this was more fun than chasing Sitka's tail. He joined in and the rowdy bunch were soon laying in a heap, panting.

It was hard to be depressed with such entertaining furry friends and she was soon back to her old routine. The week passed so quickly that she was surprised to see Steve's plane circling one afternoon. Was it the weekend already? She went down to pick him up and found that actually, it was only Thursday.

He didn't have anything on his calendar for Friday so had closed the office a day early and came out. He hoped she didn't mind.

He brought dinner for two, this time and they dined by candlelight in the cabin. Sitka was learning to sit up and beg for tidbits and the kittens would line up beside him, hoping for some, too.

They spent a companionable evening, talking and getting better acquainted. Then spent most of the night getting even better acquainted. It amazed Jo that the human body was capable of giving and receiving so much pleasure. Each time she thought it couldn't possibly be any better, he proved that it could and would. To think there were people in the world that didn't enjoy this. They just didn't now what they were missing.

They slept late the next morning and awoke to make lazy love before getting up and starting the day. What a marvelous way to start a day. Jo had never felt better in her whole life. The whole day seemed to go right. They worked on the pump and had it close to completion by the time they quit that evening. Just a few hours more work and it should be running. She thought it best to wait until next season to set it up, now. The mining season was almost over for this year, she wouldn't even have a month of work left, but she could do a lot of the preliminary work for an early start next year. After the pump was fixed, she would take it up to the workings and get a spot leveled out to set it up on. Steve cautioned about setting it just yet. Until she had seen how badly a small creek could glacier during the winter, it was best to leave everything high on the bank.

It was hard for her to think that the tiny little stream could ever make all the ice that Steve warned her about, but she would take his advice. It would be better to be safe than sorry.

They spent another quiet evening together and spent the night proving that each time still felt better than the one before.

The pump was fixed before noon, the next day. Steve asked Jo if she would fly to Fairbanks with him, have dinner, spend the night, then fly back home the next morning, very early. Jo wasn't sure about leaving the little animals alone, overnight. But it would be fun. She hadn't gone out on a date, since Thad had accepted Will's offer, in July. She put Sitka out to run for a little while, while she packed a small bag. She put a large pan of water for the animals and a lot of paper near the door, for Sitka. She left the radio playing, hoping the sound would deter a bear or other animal from entering the cabin. Maybe the sound would console the small pets, also.

Jo was surprised that the flight to Fairbanks only took about 40 minutes. Steven pointed out things she might like to see, from the air. The International Airport in Fairbanks seemed larger to her, as they came in for a landing. Either it was just because of being in a smaller plane or maybe her summer in the Bush had changed her perspective on things.

Steve owned a bachelor home in the hills that surround Fairbanks and Jo couldn't help but laugh at the elaborate seduction scene his bedroom presented.

"Do you actually sleep there, all the time? Doesn't it get to be a bit much, after a while?" She asked.

He had the grace to look a bit abashed and offered, "Well, it usually works pretty good. You're the first woman that's laughed and yes, it is a bit much. It's expected of me, I think, to live up to the image of the swinging single attorney. There is another bedroom, if you'd rather not sleep in here."

"I've never been in a 'passion pit" before, why don't we try it out? Maybe I'll learn something. Who was your decorator, Brothels'R'Us?"

She brought her lone dress and strappy little heels so took a quick shower, dressed and then brushed her hair out into a rippling curtain. She had two antique combs that she used to pull her hair back from her face with. She had some makeup in her purse, so applied some eye makeup and lip gloss. A small spray of perfume finished her preparations and she was ready to go. As she came out of the bathroom, Steve let out a low whistle.

"Lady, you are beautiful. I'll have to be careful or someone will steal you away."

Jo had never been told she was even pretty, let alone beautiful and didn't quite know how to accept such a compliment. One look at his face told her that he meant what he said. She caught a reflection of herself in the full length mirror on his closet door. She did look almost beautiful.

He had used the other bathroom and was ready to go, also. He called and made reservations at a small family run restaurant a few miles out of Fairbanks for their dinner. The drive out was nice and she was able to see a bit of the scenery surrounding Fairbanks before it got too dark to make out.

The restaurant was a lovely log building, the setting very rustic. The menu was surprising for such a small place and she left the selection up to Steve. He was more familiar with what was offered. The meal was delicious. After they had eaten, he drove slowly back to Fairbanks.

"Would you like to make an evening of it? Go somewhere and listen to a band and dance or go to a movie? There are several movies playing and there is bound to be at least one good one, somewhere. Or we could rent a movie and watch it at my place?" He twirled an imaginary mustache and leered at her under his wriggling eyebrows in a Groucho Marx imitation.

They decided to dance a while, then see what they felt like doing, from there. She already knew what she felt like doing, but figured she shouldn't just baldly state what was on her mind. Besides, she didn't get to have a night out on the town with a distinguished escort, every night. Might as well take advantage of it, while she had the chance.

The evening passed in a whirl of music and dancing. She never lacked a partner and could have danced all night, if she had been so inclined. A couple of the fellows even asked her for her phone number. But when Steve asked if she wanted to stay longer, she was more than ready to go back to the house. He pulled her close to him, as he drove and the fingers on the hand that was across the back of the seat were starting to work their magic along her neck.

By the time they reached his house, they were both feeling slightly intoxicated with each other. She decided two could play that game with the magic fingers and he was as on fire as she was.

They went straight to the bedroom and she wasn't a bit surprised to find this was a waterbed. The velvet and satin cover felt wonderful against her bare skin. She was also not surprised to find the sheets were satin. So this was what was expected of the swinging bachelor, was it? As soon as they sat on the bed, soft music started and subdued lighting came on to softly illuminate the room. Ve-r-r-ry good. There was bound to be a small refrigerator or cooler near to hand, with a bottle of chilled wine, shouldn't there? She mentioned this to him and he had the grace to blush a bit and admit that yes, there was. He showed her the panel on the headboard that swung back to reveal a small unit. She certainly wasn't bowled over by all of this, was she, he thought. But then other thoughts filled their minds and they proceeded to delight in each other. The waterbed was okay, but tended to ripple a wave at the wrong timing. But it was comfortably warm to sleep on. Morning came much too early, but she had to get back to the cabin. They reluctantly left the bed and had a quick breakfast before leaving for the airport. He wanted to know if she needed anything at a store, before they went back and she thought it would be nice to get some fresh fruit. They stopped at a large supermarket and she made her purchases quickly.

While in the store, she spotted a CD/tape player that ran on batteries so got it, with some tapes and CDs and spare batteries. There was also a selection of mitts, hats and scarves, so she bought some of those, also. It would not be long before she needed much more than that. Steve offered to bring her in one morning in a couple of weeks so she could shop all day for winter gear, then fly her back out that evening. She accepted his kind offer, it would certainly be easier than herding the old pickup into town for supplies.

The flight back to the airstrip was a bit bumpy as the weather was not being very agreeable. Large thunderclouds were rolling up and made rough air pockets. They landed smoothly and Steve told her he had best get right back to town before the weather closed in. Her old pickup was parked at the edge of the airstrip, so she loaded her supplies and drove back to the cabin.

Chapter 16

Sitka, Toolik and Atigun greeted her as though she had been gone at least a week. The cabin looked like it, too. She proceeded to clean up the mess and fed the animals. The weather forecast was for light frost to hit that night, so she spent most of the day harvesting the vegetables that frost would damage. She covered some of the plants to prolong the harvest time. If the weather held true to form, it would freeze one or two nights, then warm up for another couple of weeks. Might as well extend the garden production as long as possible. Soon there would be no fresh vegetables. She dug up some leaf lettuce plants and brought them into the cabin to see how they would fare on a window sill. The rest she covered.

With the August rains, her mining had been increasing to almost twice as long per day as she had been getting through the rest of the summer. She cleaned the top riffles every day, after working, to assure that no one else did. There was still evidence once in a while that someone else had been fooling around her sluice box. Cigarette butts on the ground and large boot tracks were found, several times, during the summer. It made her nervous to think someone was watching what she was doing. It was rather like someone keeping an eye on a person's bank statements.

When she went to Fairbanks for supplies, she would have to inquire about selling her gold. Harlan and Thad would know buyers in town.

The time passed swiftly and it seemed there were never enough hours in each day to finish what needed done. She was cutting firewood every day and hauling two or three loads to the cabin. She wanted at least 15 cord on hand. It would be better to have too much than not enough. At 40 or 50 below zero, she did not want to have to go cut firewood. The bark, peeled from the birch trees, made an excellent fire starter material. So she peeled several of the trees she fell for firewood to have the bark on hand. She filled the little back shed on the cabin with wood so in case of really bad weather, illness or extreme cold, she would not have to go outside for firewood very often.

She pulled the tomato plants and hung them by their roots in the shop. The green tomatoes continued to ripen too fast, so she moved them down to the cellar. She made window boxes to put on the inside in the windows and transplanted some more lettuce and some kale to have as fresh for as long as possible for it to grow. She knew that the shorter daylight hours would soon make the plants too spindly but at least she would enjoy salads a bit longer. The cabbages were pulled, the roots washed and buried in a bin of sand in the cellar. The onions were not ready to dry, but the weather wouldn't wait, so she braided to tops and hung the ropes of onions on nails like garlands along the ridgepole of the cabin. The potatoes, turnips and carrots were dug, dried off and stored in their bins in the cellar.

It gave her a sense of pride to know that no matter what, she would have enough food to last over the winter and most of next summer. The leaves had all turned golden with a few red accents here and there, almost overnight. It was cool enough now that a small fire in the stove felt good during the day when she came in from working. She had bought a hunting license in the little village and as soon as the season opened, she would try to get a moose. But since she had not been here a year yet, it would be very expensive to get a tag, so maybe she would just buy meat in Fairbanks and plan on a moose next year.

Steve sent a message on the radio program to expect him the next morning, so she was waiting at the airstrip when he landed. He brought out several bags of food for the animals so they hauled them up to the cabin then went back to fly into Fairbanks.

She called Lorraine as soon as she got to Fairbanks and since Lorraine didn't have a class until that afternoon, she came over and picked Jo up. Steve had to work all day, but would be free early enough for them to get a bite to eat before flying back out to the cabin. Lorraine and Jo took Jo's gold to a business in town that bought gold. The man made jewelry from the nuggets, so he gave Jo a very good price for her small collection of them. The finer gold was bought at that days' spot price, minus 20%. Most gold in the area had silver and other trace elements in it, plus the man's commission. Jo was amazed at how big the check was that the man handed her. She cashed it and deposited most into her account. She kept out enough to buy what she needed to take back, today, and to buy fuel for the winter. She would need several propane bottles filled for the stove and the lights. She could get them filled at the village. She had left enough money with Steve to buy as much food as she thought the animals would need, earlier, so that was already taken care of.

Lorraine and Jo spent the rest of the morning shopping for winter gear. Jo bought several pairs of wool pants. Also some thermal underwear, socks, shirts, insulated pants to wear over her other clothes some winter insulated boots and a pair she could wear with Grampa's cross country skis. The skis were a bit too long, but she could make do with them. She would use Grampa's trapper hat, parka an over mitts. She also bought one of the foam facemasks. Being by herself, she would not know if the telltale white spots of frostbite appeared on her face. Grampa also had snowshoes and she would have to learn how to use them. She thought she would probably need a foam pillow for her bottom, if she actually did use the skis and snowshoes. She didn't think she would have time to get bored, there was too much to learn.

The women had lunch, then Lorraine had to go to classes. Jo used Steve's car to look for the bulk sales store where she would order her main winter food. Lorraine had shown her where it was, but it didn't seem to be quite where she thought it was. A friendly pedestrian finally pointed out that she was only a couple of blocks from it.

She made out a list from the catalogue that Thad had just received in the mail. The pages had tear off strips with the catalogue number written on it and space to write the quantity desired. She handed the list to the counterperson and was told it would be ready to pick up at 4:30 p.m., she signed up on their mailing list and left.

The rest of the afternoon she just wandered around town, looking at the variety of things there were to do. Then she found a couple of book stores and the afternoon passed too swiftly. She found some books on engine repairs and one on welding. There were some on mining and a couple on living in the Bush. She hoped Steve's plane would hold all the stuff she had bought, today.

She picked Steve up at 4 and they went over to get her groceries. Steve's car was well loaded by the time they got everything in it. When they unloaded the stuff at the airplane, it made quite a mound. Steve carefully loaded the supplies in, always keeping an eye on the center of balance on his plane. Everything fit and she thought there was room for more. But Steve told her that they were getting close to the weight limit that he could safely fly at. The weight was more important than the space.

They bought something to eat as they flew, so that they would have time to unload and he could still take off in the light. Landing in Fairbanks after dark would not be a problem, but he didn't want to cut it too fine on the taking off in the dark on the dirt strip.

Chapter 17

When she arrived at the cabin, the door and wall looked like it had been raked with sharp knives. A large bear had tried to get in, half heartedly or he would have made it, but had left his mark all over the outside.

Sitka, Atigun and Toolik were under the bed when Jo went into the cabin and didn't want to come out. She coaxed them and finally they scooted up close to her and stayed right at her feet all the time she was packing her supplies in. Steve had taken off after helping her load her stuff from the plane into her pickup, but the light was fading fast. So she had to unload and pack everything into her cabin and cellar. The bear tracks were very large and if it had tried much harder, it would have been into the cabin. The way the animals were acting led her to believe that the bear was still near, so she was very cautious as she unloaded the pickup. It would be dangerous to do otherwise. She slipped her pistol into the waistband of her jeans and set the shotgun by the door.

She was carrying the last armload of bags into the cabin when Sitka started growling low in his throat. She carefully turned looking at everything as she did, there, on the other side of the truck, was the large black bear. He was moving slowly toward her, swaying his huge head back and forth, sniffing the air. He had been eating well, preparing for winter hibernation.

His fur was sleek and shiny, rippling as he slowly walked toward her. She slowly backed toward the cabin door, trying not to make any sudden moves. He suddenly stood up on his hind legs, peering nearsightedly at her, then dropped to all fours and came around the front of the pickup. He clicked his teeth as he came on toward her, with one hand, she felt behind her for the shotgun. There! Her hand closed on the gun and swung it around in front of her. The bear was only about 20 feet from her as it swung it's head to the side, she dropped the bag she still carried and shot the bear just under the ear.

The bear dropped like a stone and so did she. Her legs wouldn't hold her another minute. Sitting there, she made sure there was another slug in the shotgun and watched the bear. It didn't move, suddenly a leg twitched and she shot it again, then felt foolish as it was only a spasm. The bear was definitely dead. Well, she would rather be safe than sorry. Now she would have to butcher it out. That was too nice a hide to waste, and since there were no salmon streams nearby, the meat might be good, too.

She had just finished skinning the bear and was starting to cut up the meat when Thad stopped by.

"Well, nothing like getting your meat close to the door. That way you don't have to pack it very far.

Now why didn't I ever think of that. Was it hard to get him to follow you home? That's one fine looking hunk of meat. You'll get a lot of lard from him, too. Are you okay?"

Jo assured him she was okay, just scared. He told her she had a right to be scared, the only people in this area ever killed or hurt by bears, it had been black bears that did it. Usually the grizzlies stayed away from humans, but the blacks learned that people usually leave good garbage. Even though she was careful with garbage, he may have found food around some other cabin and just checked hers, out of habit.

Jo had spread sheets of plastic around the bear, before starting to butcher, so even though it was almost at her door, there would be no bloody mess left, after she was done. The entrails were put in a tub to haul away, later. Thad helped her hang the quarters of meat in the big shop. It would be cool there and no bugs to bother. The bugs were almost gone now because of the freezing nights, but she didn't want to spoil the meat through neglect. She liberally salted the hide and rolled it up. They placed it in the shop, also. Tomorrow she could start scraping it clean. The salt would make it easier to clean, besides starting to cure it. She thought she would probably cure the shoulders and hams just like pork, Grampa had an old smokehouse out back, she would smoke the hams after they cured.

Thad sat and visited with her quite a while. He would be leaving in a few days. He was going

"Outside" for a few months to visit family. He also was going to try his hand at some of that desert prospecting. Imagine, mining in the middle of winter.

Harlan would be moving to his cabin in the village in a week or so. Then Mike and his dad would move to Fairbanks a week or so after that.

The next day, Jo worked on the bear hide and started the meat curing. She trimmed off most of the fat, first, getting several inches from the back and hams. She placed a large kettle on the back of the wood stove and started the fat rendering out for lard.

Bear fat makes a delicate lard for baking. It makes the most tender doughnuts, pies and pastries. The old time name for doughnut was "bear sign". Thad had estimated the bear to weigh over 400 pounds, easily. After manhandling the large pieces, Jo thought he might be underestimating it. The fur on the hide was lovely, so Jo thought she would try making herself a rug to use over the bed out of it. It would be nice to curl up in on a cold night.

Grampa's journals left a detailed account of winter preparations and Jo found that it helped her very much. She followed the schedule for maintenance of the dozer, and greased the pickup, too, while she was at it.

Changing the dozer oil was similar to doing the tractors on the ranch, she didn't have any difficulty with that. Harlan rode to the village with her when she went to get the propane tanks filled. Grampa had several of the tanks so she figured she would play it safe and fill all of them. She had enough money at the present, and didn't want to run out during cold weather. She also bought a barrel of kerosene. The poor old pickup was really loaded for the trip home. She drove slowly and made the trip without mishap. Harlan helped her unload the pickup, then she fixed a meal for them. She served some of the pickled vegetables from the garden, that she had made with some of the ripe tomatoes. Harlan was surprised to find the pickles delicious. Cauliflower, carrots, onions and string beans fixed like dill pickles were a novelty. Jo explained that she loved pickles and since there were no cucumbers and she had a large crop of the rest, she just experimented.

Harlan tried to think of any problems that might arise that she wasn't expecting and explained how the winters usually went. There usually would be about 2 weeks of intense cold, followed by 2 weeks or more of milder weather, still minus zero, but not extreme. Of course, there were always those exceptions. He decided there probably wasn't any usual winters and she should just be prepared for anything. He thought she had shown a lot of sense so far and was level headed and doubted she would go off the deep end over some solitude or cold weather. He renewed his offer of a place to stay at his cabin in the village, if she felt like coming to town during the winter.

After he left, she thought what a wonderful friend

he was. He had a very small cabin in the village and she knew she would be crowding him if she took up the offer to stay. But he meant it when he offered her the cabin. She was welcome to what he had.

It was cold enough now that she thought she would clean the sluice box the next day. Then she would close down for the season. She thought she would intensively cut firewood for the next couple of weeks. She had about 12 cord of wood cut and stacked in the woodshed, but more could always be burned next year. She started stacking some in the shop in all empty spaces. She might want to work in there or warm up the old pickup, to drive somewhere, although she wasn't sure whether the roads were kept open or not. There was an old snowplow that attached to the pickup, but she didn't think she wanted to try plowing all the way to the village or to Fairbanks. She doubted if she could, even if she wanted to. The old pickup had two large gas tanks, but plowing takes a lot of gas. She would just have to plan on staying here, once the roads were snowed in. It should be quite a winter.

Chapter 18

Jo had not started a journal when she first got to Alaska. But decided she would write down as much as she remembered from her trip North to the present and try to remember to write in it every day from now on.

When she arrived at the sluice box the next day, it was obvious that someone had been there before her. The upper riffles were pulled out of the box and laying on the ground by the box. Luckily, she had continued cleaning the upper riffles every day.

Whoever had done it, quit after not finding anything in the upper end of the box. She proceeded to clean the rest of the box and found some nuggets and fine gold farther down the box. It would be a nice nest egg for start-up next summer.

She shut the water off, going into the pipe through the dam. Then she cut the dam with the dozer to route the water around the boxes. When she got the dozer back to the cabin, she cleaned the tracks and undercarriage. Now it would be ready to start up and use, if she had to, during the winter if it wasn't too cold.

She noticed autumn was a brief affair, lasting only a week or so. According to Grampa's journals, spring was just as brief. There were basically two seasons in Alaska, summer and winter. Winter just hogged more than it's share of the year. Now, at the end of September, there was less than 12 hours of sunlight per day and the trees were all bare of leaves.

After reading one of the books she had bought about Bush living, she put a small stove she found in a shed into the little bunkhouse. Then she stored some bedding, clothing and a supply of dry food. If there were ever a fire in her cabin, she would still have a place to stay until she was able to go to town. She also stored some of the dry goods in a barrel in the shop. It gave her more room in her cabin, having this bulky stuff stored elsewhere.

Mice were moving into the cabin by the bunch. Actually, they were red-backed Voles, but they looked like short eared mice and acted like mice. Atigun and Toolik surprised themselves and her by catching several. Sitka soon joined in and the three of them managed to reduce the mouse population considerably. She took them to the other buildings and sheds and let them have at the mice. Several days of this and the mouse population was nil around the buildings.

Steve sent several messages on the radio program to her. He was tied up in town, then when he had the time, the weather had not cooperated. Will and Lorraine sent her some messages too, so Jo heard from someone almost every night. She wasn't able to answer them, but she did start letters to everyone. Whenever someone went to town, she would send the letters in to be mailed. Two of the radio stations had regular times of the day that they broadcast messages to people living in the Bush. It was looked forward to by the people in the Bush and sometimes was like listening in on an old party line. She knew the names of families living all around her that she had never met. She even knew what rivers or streams they lived on, from the messages. She started tying small weights to Sitka's harness and he dragged them all over the place. He thought it was a new game and entered into it wholeheartedly. The kittens followed, pouncing on the weight and letting him pull them around, too. He was a sled dog at heart and loved pulling.

That was good as she had plans for him this winter. If she could figure out skiing, he could pull her on the skis. She thought this would be sort of a case of the blind leading the blind, since she had never skied and he had never pulled anything but kittens. She never trained a dog before, either, but he seemed to take to this naturally. She hoped she did, as well. If determination counted, she could do it.

Mike and his father stopped by to say goodbye an found her in the shop while Sitka pulled Atigun and Toolik around the yard on a large piece of bark. They thought it was really something to see a dog and cats getting along so well. In truth, the animals probably thought they were related, having been raised together.

They all went inside and had some coffee and sweets she had baked yesterday. She had had another attack of chocoholica and made a batch of fudge. She wrapped some for them to take with them. She was going to have to learn to cook smaller amounts or freeze a lot of stuff, when colder weather hit. All she would have to do would be to set something on her back room shelf. Or outdoors, it would freeze in short order.

She sealed all the letters she had been writing and sent them in with Mike to be mailed. She decided to go to the village before the end of the week and pick up any mail she might have. She also had some requests to send for catalogues that she wanted to receive from several companies. Junk mail was better than no mail at all.

A couple of days later she awoke to lazy snowflakes starting to fall from a leaden sky. She decided if she were going to the village, this would have to be the day. The night before, she had started new letters to everyone. She hurriedly finished them and started the old pickup. She thought for good measure, she should buy one more barrel of gasoline so put a barrel in the back of the pickup. She took the shotgun with her, loaded with birdshot. The grouse were filling their crops with gravel from the road and she could use a "chicken" dinner.

The Postmaster was surprised to hear that she was

staying, then smiled and said he didn't know why it surprised him. She was Jeremy's granddaughter. He told her that if she came to the village during the winter and needed a place to spend the night before starting back out to her cabin, she could stay with him and his wife. His wife came in just after he said that and said the same thing. It made Jo feel good that these people accepted her into their lives so easily. The friendliness of almost everyone she met in Alaska still amazed her. Too bad people weren't like this everywhere.

She bought her barrel of gasoline, then splurged and bought herself a shrimp dinner at the roadhouse. They were getting ready to close down for the winter. The owner was complaining about the difficulty he had finding someone to do his baking for him in the summer. He and Jo talked for a while and she offered to come down and bake once a week. If he needed more, she could maybe make it twice a week. They worked out a rate of pay satisfactory to both of them. He would supply her gas for the trip and pay so much per hour. He waved her money away when she tried to pay for her dinner and told her it was on the house. She thanked him and drove home.

There had been quite a stack of mail for her at the Post Office. She had glanced through them, but wouldn't open any until she got home. She had tried to call her folks but there was no answer at their home.

She got three grouse along the road on her way

home. They would be tomorrows dinner.

When she got to the cabin, the snow was still lazily falling. A slight breeze was blowing and the snow swirled in little eddys along the edge of the road. There was no accumulation yet, but there would be, soon.

She was cleaning the grouse when she heard a vehicle pull up out in the yard. When she answered the door she was surprised to see Steve standing there, smiling at her. He hugged and kissed her soundly, then asked how she had been and if she had missed him.

She had been too busy to miss anyone and told him so. He told her she had mortally wounded his ego. He had been sure she was pining away for him. He risked life and limb to drive all the way out here and she had hardly missed him? Oh, he might never recover from the agony of it all. So... what did she have planned for tonight? Any thing that could be put off until tomorrow? She told him that she had planned on working on her bear hide, then grinned. He said, "Bare hide? What are you going to do to your bare hide?:"

"You'll just have to wait and see, won't you?" She answered sweetly.

With visions of erotic possibilities dancing in his mind, he was sadly disappointed later, when she unfolded the bear skin to work on. He was amazed when she told him how she had gotten it. The fur was so soft and luxurious, he once again started to have thoughts of the possibilities the fur presented.

The evening passed swiftly, they talked about what
the winter would be like, everyone they knew and
where they were all spending the winter, everything
except talk about themselves. Finally he could stand
the suspense no longer and moved closer to her.
His fingers started their magic along her neck and
around her ear. She pretended to ignore him,
scraping the hide with a metal tool. Her breath gave
her away, as it quickened. He blew little puffs of
warm air around her ear as his fingers worked their
way around the neckline of her shirt and started
down the front. Soon he was nibbling kisses in the
path of his fingers and she gave up all pretense and
reciprocated his attentions. Soon the bear fur was
the only thing between her and the couch, it's fur
both sensuous and tickly on her skin. The gas light
cast shadows on the walls as they made slow
delicious love.

The weekend passed quickly, the weather remained
cold, with little flurries of snow. Jo and Steve found
a well point and casing in the shop and an old
pitcher pump, still in it's box, under the workbench.
Grampa had mentioned pounding down a well,
from the cellar, so he could have water in the winter
without having to pack it or melt snow.

So Steve offered to help and they cleared an area
in the cellar, near the drain for the sink. They made
a driver for the casing from an old dozer roller and
welded handles on it. Then they positioned the well
point and started driving. By the time they were
down 20 feet, they both had discovered muscles they

hadn't used before. Even though they were both in good physical condition, they knew they would be sore the next day.

They thought they hit water at 25 feet, but went a bit further, just in case. They cut a hole in the floor, under the kitchen counter and one through the counter and placed the casing up through it. Jo poured part of a bottle of bleach down the pipe to sterilize it and settle the water. They attached the pump and primed it with a pitcher of water.

Nothing happened. They waited a while and primed the pump again. This time water came up, They were a success. The water smelled strongly of the bleach, so they dumped it back down. Tomorrow they would pump out several gallons, if possible and see if the water was any good. Even if it wasn't the best quality of water, she could use it for washing and cleaning. She could always get drinking water from the little spring near the creek. It would be nice not to have to haul all her water though, especially in extreme cold, when she would have to chop through deep ice or search for overflow for water.

To celebrate the new well, they heated all the water she had drained from the rainwater tanks outside the cabin for bathing. There was a large oval wash tub hanging in the back room, that they filled with the hot water. It was a tight fit, but they both managed to squeeze into it. They bathed each other, then stood and poured fresh warm water over each other to rinse off the soap. They slipped on their shoes and carried the tub out to the other side of the road and dumped it. They ran laughing back into the cabin, the cold air raising Goosebumps on their wet nude bodies. They figured if anyone had happened to drive up just then, they would be certified as loonies, running around in below freezing temperatures in only their shoes.

As they re-entered the cabin, their laughter turned to fear as they saw that their horsing around had managed to knock something flammable too close to the wood stove and was now burning near the wall. Panic overtook reason for a couple of minutes as they tried to pump up some water to throw on the fire. Then they remembered that a pump has to be primed, to work. Jo poured a pitcher of water down the pump and Steve pumped furiously. Soon they had the fire out, but they were much more subdued than they had been minutes before. It would have been very easy to have lost everything in just a few minutes of carelessness.

They moved everything away from the stove and cleaned up the mess. They had thrown on whatever clothes they could find and as they finished the cleanup, they looked at each other and laughed. He had her shirt and she, his. Buttons were missing or crookedly fastened. Her hair was hanging in stringy strands from the knot she had fastened on top her head before their bath. A streak of soot was across her face, which she smeared more, trying to push her hair back. He reached over to wipe it off and left more, with his sooty fingers.

They washed up and collapsed on the bed. The evening hadn't turned out like either had planned. She had decided to practice her feminine wiles on him and see how he responded to being seduced. She thought he might enjoy it, but wasn't sure. She also wasn't too sure of her own abilities yet, but didn't think he would mind being practiced on. They might both enjoy the end results. So she started in.

When he figured out what she was doing, he turned to her, groaned, held his hand to his forehead and said, "Not tonight, Dear, I have a headache."

She promptly set out to prove she was the best cure for a headache and before long, he wholeheartedly agreed.

Steve decided it was best to leave a little early, Sunday afternoon. The snow was starting to fall in earnest and the high passes between the cabin and town might blow drifts too deep for his car to break through.

After he left, the cabin seemed rather empty, but that didn't last long. There was still too much to do, to sit and feel alone.

The water still had a chlorine smell, but not so much and had proven to be a fair quantity. It would supply all her needs, anyway, and she was glad to have the well. She had planned to work on it in small amounts, every day. But since Steve had been willing to work, she wasn't going to tell him to quit. They both had noticed the sore muscles, this morning as they stretched on awakening. But it wasn't as bad as she was expecting. They massaged each other's sore shoulders and soon forgot all sore muscles.

Chapter 19

Her days settled into a routine of work and studying. She cut wood every morning and hauled it until noon. Then she played with Sitka in the snow, teaching him to pull on command. Atigun and Toolik didn't care much for the snow and would sit in the windowsill looking out at them in disgust. She started strapping on the skis and was soon able to maneuver around quite well in them. Of course, the snow was only a few inches deep so maybe that helped.

The snowshoes were more awkward to learn to walk in. She had to swing her legs around as she walked to keep from hitting the snowshoe on her other leg. Sitka loved the snow and did not like having to come back in the cabin after they were done for the day. He went with her on her wood cutting trips and was learning to respond to verbal commands.

The late afternoons and evenings, she studied in the books she had bought and that Grampa had left. She had set a course of study for herself and was trying to stick to it. She wrote in her journal every day and usually would write in an on-going letter she started to her family. It would be the size of a book by spring.

The weather warmed up a bit and some of the snow melted, but not all of it. Then the temperature dropped. She decided one more trip to the village for mail was in order, so planned to go the next day. She wasn't sure how well the old pickup would start at below zero temperatures, so built a fire in the barrel stove in the shop. It would keep the pickup warm all night, so she wouldn't have to worry.

The day dawned bright, clear and cold. It was 23 below zero on the thermometer and only the end of October. It didn't feel that cold to her, but she believed the thermometer, so dressed accordingly. It would probably not be possible to get to the Post Office just before Christmas, so she wrapped the few purchases she had made during the summer trips to Fairbanks for her family for Christmas. She added some of the lingonberry and blueberry jellies she had made, marked the package Do Not Open Until Christmas. She doubted that Sue could stand the suspense, but Mom would keep it put up. It just depended on who got the mail the day the package arrived.

The pickup started right away and she made the drive with no problem. Once she got on the main road, it appeared to have been well used and the snow was packed solid in the places it still covered the road.

The Postmaster and his wife invited her to their cabin for lunch so she stayed and visited until time to close for lunch. It was nice to talk to someone, for a change. Sitka, Atigun and Toolik were fine companions but the conversation was limited. She had a lot of mail, some of the catalogues were already arriving and she had gotten on some of the junk mailing lists so she would always have something in her mail. Her family had written several letters, which she would read, at the cabin.

She called them on the phone, but it was really chilly out so that conversation was really brief. Everyone was fine. Bill's ranch had sold to a nice young couple. They still sounded wistful about Bill, but she couldn't help it. She just felt relief that she wasn't ever going to have to see Bill Humphries again.

She enjoyed a pleasant lunch with the Postmaster and his wife and left soon after to get back to the cabin before dark. The daylight hours were getting very brief and losing 6 to 8 minutes a day. By December 21, there would be only 2 to 3 hours of sunlight, several hours of twilight, though.

Time continued to pass swiftly. She was surprised to discover that Thanksgiving was only a couple of days away. She decided to hunt for a grouse or rabbit to have for Thanksgiving dinner and make a change in her diet. The bear hams and shoulders had turned out rather well but a person got tired of eating the same thing every day. She had canned meat in the cellar, but wanted to use the fresh meat first. She had baked, broiled, fried, barbequed and everything else she could think of to do to the meat, but it was still bear meat. She even ground up part of it and made sausage. Next year, she would definitely have to get a moose. Grampa had left quite a bit of canned moose meat so she did have some on hand. It was very good meat, but she didn't want to use it all up too fast.

There had been several small snow storms and there was about a foot of snow on the ground. She finally figured out how to attach the snowplow to the pickup and plowed her road down to the main road after each snowfall. She decided to wear her cross country skis and go hunting up the hill behind her cabin. Sitka was sadly disappointed to have to stay at the cabin when she left. He was beginning to look forward to their excursions with the skis. She knew there would be no hunting with his company. His puppy exuberance still overcame his ability to follow commands when he became exited.

She had gone about a half mile from the cabin when she came across a set of tracks made by snowshoes. They came from the opposite direction and angled across the trail she was following. Someone else must be out looking for a Thanksgiving dinner, also, she thought. She continued on in the direction she had been going and thought no more about the tracks. There was a homesteader that lived on the next hill over, everyone had warned her that they wanted privacy and did not take kindly to friendly neighbors.

A little farther along the trail, she saw a huge Arctic hare. She couldn't believe her eyes, rabbits don't get that big. But there it was, bigger than life, right off the edge of the trail. She shot it and still could not believe how big it was. It must have weighted close to 20 pounds. She would find out later that Arctic Hares could get even larger than the one she shot, but it would make a lovely Thanksgiving dinner. She had made cranberry sauce from the low bush cranberries or lingonberries and would make a dressing and stuff the rabbit like a turkey. Sitka, Atigun and Toolik had better appreciate this, she thought.

When she returned to the cabin, she cleaned the rabbit and soaked it in water with baking soda added. This would remove any gamey taste from the rabbit's diet. She cleaned and stretched the skin. It might come in handy later, it was very soft.

She was finally happy with her supply of firewood. With almost 20 cord stacked in the woodshed, around the cabin and shop, she had a good supply. She had a cellar full of food and was in good health, she would really have a lot to be thankful for on Thanksgiving.

Chapter 20

Thanksgiving day dawned bright and clear, almost halfway through the day. Since snow had fallen, there was never total darkness, but it was too dark most of the time to work well without extra light. The sun actually came above the horizon at about 10:30 a.m. and would set about 2:30 or 3 p.m. The rabbit was slow baking in the Dutch oven on the wood stove. There was a pumpkin pie cooling on the counter and the odors drifting around the cabin had Sitka, Atigun and Toolik all walking around, sniffing the air and drooling.

She was surprised to hear a vehicle pull up in her yard about noon. She was even more surprised to see Lorraine and Mike getting out of it. Mike carried a large box as they came to the door and Lorraine could hardly keep from dancing around. Jo opened the door and Lorraine almost knocked her down in her happiness at seeing her again. Sitka was excited at seeing his pals again, so everyone was a tangle for a moment or two.

Mike said Lorraine wouldn't give him a moments

peace until he agreed to come out. Will could not come due to prior commitments but sent his best wishes.

They had brought a small baked turkey with them and assorted fresh vegetables and a relish tray already fixed up. As they unpacked the box, there was a familiar sound of a plane buzzing the cabin. They all went out to look and the plane circled low, again, then headed for the airstrip. Mike handed Jo the keys to his pickup and she went down to pick up Steve.

When she arrived at the airstrip, Steve was draining the oil from the plane into a bucket. He snapped a lid on the bucket and put it in the back of the pickup. Then he started unloading boxes from the back of the plane. He, too, had brought a small baked turkey and a dinner with all possible trimmings. There would certainly be enough food for everyone.

"I'm not going to ask if you missed me, my ego couldn't stand the answer." Steve told her.

But she had missed him, she had missed all of them. That was the trouble, she missed them all in equal amounts. Steve was special but not indispensable. She liked him very much, more than enjoyed their love life, but when he wasn't here, she seldom even thought of him. What was wrong with her, anyway, here was a wonderful fellow, thoughtful, kind, probably even wonderful and she wasn't in love with him. Had the fiasco with Bill given her a jaundiced outlook on love? She hoped not.

Actually, she missed not having Will here, with them. She must have a jaundiced outlook, she wasn't even sure she liked Will and he was certainly not her type. A little voice asked her, so? What is your type, Bill? This was ridiculous, pretty soon she would not only be talking to herself, she would be answering, then saying Huh? What'd you say? She was shaking her head when Steve walked around the end of the pickup.

"What's the matter? Loosing an argument with yourself?" He asked.

She jumped, then blushed, he was very close to the truth. He gave her a big hug and a more than friendly kiss and they got in the pickup. He wanted to know what all she had been doing since he seen her last. She quickly told him and asked about his goings on since last they'd met.

He told her it was just more of the same old thing. Work, which was interesting and work that wasn't. She teased him about keeping up his swinging single image and he told her it was harder to do, since she had laughed at his 'passion pit'. Somehow he always thought of that at the wrong times. She was glad he wasn't taking their relationship seriously, now she could relax and just enjoy him while he was with her.

As soon as they unpacked the boxes Steve had brought, they started doing some serious eating. The rabbit was done perfectly and the sage/cashew nut dressing was enjoyed by everyone. Everyone ate too much and they spent the afternoon and evening lazing around on the couch, talking and listening to music.

Everyone brought sleeping bags, so instead of trying to heat up the little bunkhouse, everyone opted for sleeping on the floor of the warm cabin. It was now about 40 below zero F. out by the time they went to bed and dropping fast.

The next morning, the temperature was a frigid minus 62 degrees F. The cabin was warm and cozy but no one wanted to go outside. Mike hoped it would warm up a bit by Sunday as he had to be back in town Monday morning for work. Steve told him that if necessary, he could fly back in with him, then fly back out to get the truck when the cold spell broke.

They read, ate, played cribbage, ate and in the evening started a spirited game of poker. Lorraine had never played and Jo only filled in at one of Bill's poker sessions, so of course the men kept trying to change the rules to suit whatever they happened to be playing at the moment. Lorraine ended the evening the big winner with the largest pile of beans at the table. She ended up 200 lima beans, 34 pinto beans an 74 navy beans ahead.

Saturday, everyone helped pull and stretch the bear hide to soften it. They took numerous snack breaks and no one seemed the least bit hungry when Jo asked if they wanted her to fix dinner. Somehow, she wasn't hungry either, so they proceeded to snack their way through the evening. Mike and Steve demanded the right to win back their beans, so they had another game of poker to end the evening.

Lorraine shared the bed with Jo, Steve said his advanced age gave him the rights to the couch, Mike smiled and said okay and when Steve tried to get comfortable on the couch, he knew why. He had the couch alright, but Mike had the cushions under him, on the floor.

By noon, Sunday, the weather had warmed to about minus 30 degrees F, so Mike decided to try warming up the truck and driving back to Fairbanks. There was an old weed burner that used propane, in Jo's shop, so he found some lengths of stove pipe and an elbow of pipe, put them together and aimed the open elbow up under his oil pan. He started the weed burner and aimed the flame towards the open end of the pipe.

Everyone helped place sheets of plywood around the truck to help hold the heat in under it. Then they all went back inside to stay warm. Mike had plenty of Arctic gear in the truck, in case of a breakdown on the road, and Jo packed a box with food for them to eat on the way back to town. They had a couple of thermos bottles that she filled with boiling water. They had instant coffee, tea and soup that they could make with it.

Steve was heating his bucket of oil on the wood stove to put back in the plane for his trip to town.

Mike's pickup started right up as soon as he went out to try it. He had two heavy duty batteries and winter weight oil and lube in it, too. So he and Lorraine were soon on their way.

Jo took Steve down to the plane and waited while

he poured the warm oil back in and started the engine. He had a similar box she had packed for him of food to have along the way or in case he had to emergency land. He also had Arctic gear and survival rations in the plane but hot water and fresh food would be welcome in an emergency. His takeoff was smooth and he circled her then headed toward Fairbanks. She knew the weekend had not gone exactly as he had planned, but he enjoyed himself anyway.

It really had been quite a Thanksgiving weekend and she had not had time to sit and miss her family. This was her first holiday ever, away from them. Steve had more letters to mail from her to her family. He had offered to fly her to the village for her mail but she knew it would soon be dark and wanted him to be either landed at Fairbanks or close to it, by dark.

When she got back to the cabin, she noticed a box on her couch that she hadn't seen before. It must have been set aside when they packed everything in. When she opened it, she found it contained brightly wrapped Christmas presents. There was a note from Lorraine, explaining that since they didn't know if they would be able to make it back before Christmas, they had left these in the truck until just before they left. She was not to open them until Christmas. She placed the box in the back shed and sat down and cried. She wasn't sure why she was crying, but the thoughtfulness of her friends just seemed to overwhelm her.

The pets crowded around her and tried to console her as best they could. Soon she had about all the tears she could stand, hugged them all and started cleaning up the cabin.

She had messages the next night on the radio, letting her know that everyone made the trip to town okay. She started new letters to everyone and tried to think of something she could make for each of her friends for Christmas.

She had stretched and dried the rabbit hide, so it was ready to tan. She started on it immediately. Lorraine had loved her trappers hat, she could make one for Lorraine from the rabbit, unless she could find something else. She had a velvet blouse that would do fine for the rest of the hat. It would go well with Lorraine's coloring, the white rabbit fur with the darker undercoat and the burgundy velvet. She would line the hat with some quilted lining she had from an old jacket. She would put elastic across the back of the hat so it would fit any size head. She hoped Lorraine wouldn't mind the use of used materials in the hat. But she couldn't just run down to the store for things.

Deciding what to make for the men was a harder decision. She would have to think about that while she was working on Lorraine's hat. She made a pattern from her hat and cut out the velvet and the liner. She worked on softening the skin and sewed the material pieces together. Everything had to be sewn by hand and it took her quite a while. She worked on the hat project in her spare time for about a week and still hadn't decided what to make for the men.

Finally she decided on homemade candy. It would pack well and she could make several varieties. She started making one batch every evening. It was a good thing she had plans for this stuff, she would weigh a couple hundred pounds by the end of the winter, if she wasn't careful. She made pulled mints, fondant covered cherries dipped in chocolate, fudge and panoche. That was about the limit of the supplies she had on hand, so she peeled some birch bark from some of the larger pieces of firewood after bringing them in and thawing a bit. She made simple baskets from the bark, lined them with waxed paper then arranged the candies in layers separated by plastic wrap, in the baskets. She made laced designs on the top, also from bark.

The hat turned out pretty good and the baskets were finished. The weather warmed up to a balmy minus 15 degrees F. so she decided to see if the road was still open to the village. To her surprise, it was.

Someone had dragged a large plank behind their vehicle, it looked like. She had to drop her plow a couple of places to knock down drifts of snow but most of the road was not bad.

The Postmaster was surprised to see her and offered her a place to spend the night. She declined, saying she didn't want her fire to go out in the cabin, but thanked him for the offer. She mailed her packages to Fairbanks and was surprised to have a large package waiting, from her family.

She stopped to see Harlan for a few minutes on her way back to the cabin. He was feeling fine and asked if she wanted to stay. She declined, but thanked him, too. He said he had gotten a letter from Thad and he was fast remembering why he moved to Alaska in the first place. His relatives were driving him up the wall and the traffic was unbelievable. Lovely meadows and valleys were now paved and became towns. Everyone was in a hurry to get nowhere. Everyone thought he was made of money, being a rich Alaskan gold miner and pestered him for money or backing for harebrained schemes. One small nephew had actually asked him outright for a million dollars, "because he was old and couldn't enjoy spending it like he could."

Harlan figured Thad would be back before Christmas. Jo had made baskets of candy for Harlan and Thad, too, so left them with Harlan. She had spray painted old newspapers for wrapping paper, then cut out snow flake shapes, put them on the paper and sprayed with another color paint. The paper turned out pretty good and she teased Harlan that he could always read the inside of it.

She returned to her cabin after dark, which wasn't hard to do now, with only about 3 ½ hours of sunlight per day. She unloaded the big box from her family, then put the pickup back in the shop. It was nice to have it heated up before she had to start it. The old barrel stove did a fine job.

Time seemed to whiz by as Jo worked on her studies and the day to day chores around the cabin.

A couple of days before Christmas, she cut down a little spruce tree to decorate. She made decorations for it from paper chains cut in intricate patterns, popcorn threaded on string, bread dough shaped and baked hard, then painted with food coloring. She had a hard time convincing Sitka not to eat most of the decorations and Atigun and Toolik out of climbing the tree. It wasn't too firmly set, anyway, and she was afraid the whole works would fall over. She wrapped pieces of candy in foil and hung them on the tree, also. But Sitka wanted them so badly, she figured he would get them one way or another, so removed them from the tree.

She placed the presents from her family and friends under the tree. It looked very nice, she thought. She took some pictures of the tree with her pets around it. Then she put the camera on a box, set it and took a picture with herself and the animals around the tree. She might have cards made next year and could use one of these pictures.

There had not been any snow since her trip to the village, so she was not very surprised to see Harlan pull up in her yard on Christmas day. She was a bit more surprised though, that Thad was actually with him. The real surprise, was Will, sitting in the back seat of the old Jeep. He said he was learning to fly and had landed at the village on his cross country flight. Since Harlan was coming out here, he had sort of hitched a ride, Lorraine would want to know how she was doing.

She had fixed a nice lunch, just in case someone

just happened to show up and they all sat down to eat., with relish. She thanked them for their thoughtfulness and presents. She had opened her presents that morning. Will had made a box full of fanciful birdhouses, that he had sent out with Mike and Lorraine. There were miniature cabins and a castle for the swallows that came every year.

Mike and Lorraine sent out art supplies. She had mentioned one time to Lorraine that she would like to learn how to paint. She always doodled little animals and figures around the edges of her letters and journal pages. There were a couple of books for beginner painters, also. She hung the birdhouses on her tree, they were so darling. They added a special touch to the decorations. Will seemed embarrassed by her thanks, but she thought he was secretly pleased that she liked them so much.

Will wasn't sure why he had spent so many hours making the little houses for her, or even why he had come out here, today, with Harlan and Thad. He did always enjoy the two men's company, that must be it. He still was not sure why he felt attracted to Jo. She just was not his type of woman.

The men left soon after lunch. Will had to continue his flight back to Fairbanks.

Jo sat and looked through her new books. The art books from Mike and Lorraine and the books her family had sent her. Her mother picked out several she knew her daughter would enjoy. Her sister sent her a lovely dress that she didn't know if she would ever have an excuse to wear, but it was beautiful.

Her father had made a nice leather belt for her, that had lovely carving on it. Her little brother, Danny, had drawn a picture of the ranch house and outbuildings and framed it. She hung it on the wall of the cabin. He had done a pretty good job for only being 10 years old. Steve found a couple of old books on the early days in Alaska that he thought she would like so he bought them for her. Harlan and Thad brought her a nugget necklace, made from their own nuggets. It was made so she could add a larger nugget as a pendant at a later date. She had had a wonderful Christmas.

Chapter 21

Almost before she knew it, it was the New Year. She had been so busy with her new art supplies and with her studies, she hadn't noticed how fast the days were going by. Her friends in Fairbanks sent messages wishing her a Happy New Year. When she heard it, she discovered she had forgotten to mark the calendar. It was very easy to lose track of time, here by herself.

She followed Grampa's trail markers for his little trapline. The trail was easy to find, he had marked trees with his special little slash arrangement. She had kept the trail open and followed it on skis. She thought she might set a few traps for some furs for her own use even though it was illegal. Next year she would get a license and trap for sale. She thought that if she didn't keep the trapline showing signs of use, someone else might try taking it over.

She found signs of the snowshoer again, after the last snow. The person had come upon her trail, followed it a ways, then veered off in the direction from which he came. She thought of the snowshoer as he, but wasn't sure. The tracks were quite deep, so the person weighed more than she did, the snow was knocked off limbs that were above her head, so the person was taller than she, also.

Soon after the New Year, she took some traps and went up the trail to set them. She read all she could find on trapping and read in Grampa's journals about how he had done it. She boiled the traps in the autumn and left them hang outdoors. The gloves she wore had been boiled with them, then left hang outdoors, also. She wore other gloves, then pulled these on over, to mask her odor as much as possible.

She found the bottles of scent used to attract animals to the traps and had one in her overcoat pocket. She wanted to catch some marten, the furs would make nice hats and mitts. The trees Grampa had cut and notched were in place along the trail. She only had to attach the traps to the tree and set them. After the first one, she set them first, then attached them to the trees. She spaced the traps out along the trail. She only wanted a few and didn't want to catch them all in one area. She timed her round of the trapline, then headed home.

She started out early the next morning and was surprised to find a marten in the second trap she came to. She reset the trap and continued her round. There was one more, in the last trap. After she reset the trap, she headed back home. At this rate. It would not take long to catch all she wanted for what she wanted to make.

She skinned the marten as soon as they thawed and stretched the hides. She would start working on them tomorrow after returning from her rounds.

The next day she had nothing in her traps, but there were snowshoe tracks around her trail. Whoever it was, was keeping an eye on her trap line, also, but hadn't touched anything.

The next day, she had one marten and one trap was sprung. She reset and went back to the cabin.

In the next few days, she found one more marten, the snowshoe tracks several times and she wasn't sure, but it appeared that the snowshoer had taken one or more of the marten from her traps.

It took her almost a month to catch enough marten for her own personal use. She was sure, now, that the snowshoer had taken quite a few animals from her traps. She still hadn't seen the snowshoer, but if and when she did, she would have a few words about taking other people's property. If the person had asked, she would have given what was needed, but to take without asking, upset her.

She went around picking up her traps as soon as she had enough. She would not leave them out. As she came to the last trap, she saw a figure bent over, working at the trap. She yelled an the person whirled around. Bill! What was he doing here? She thought she had seen the last of him. But if he was the one stealing from her traps, it fit in with her image of him.

He took off, in a clumsy shuffling run, on the snowshoes. She could have easily caught him, on her skis, but then what would she do with him? She certainly didn't want him. She fired a shot into the air, to hurry him on his way. Instead, he fell, muffled curses drifting back to her, he struggled to his feet and continued on, still muttering dire curses at her. So much for the guy she once thought was her Prince Charming. She briefly wondered if the fellow that had bought her claims from Bill had ever caught up with him. Somehow she doubted it.

The pack of traps was very heavy and she wished she had brought Sitka with her, to help carry them. He was learning, fast, to be a skijor dog. The harness she had made for him had added pockets to carry things. She could attach saddlebags and used a snap leash to have him pull her on the skis. He thought this was a fine new game. He did have a tendency to go under things that knocked her flat. Then he would come back and jump on her, thinking this was all part of the game. She was teaching him Gee and Haw for left and right turns and he usually got it right. The other times were best forgotten.

By the time she returned to the cabin, she decided to write down in her journal and in letters to everyone about seeing Bill, here. She did not trust him and was afraid he would do something that would cause her harm. Where was he staying? How had he gotten back here?

She disliked having Bill in the area. How long had he been here? Could he possibly be the one stealing from her sluice box during the summer? He smoked cigarettes so maybe he was the one. She wouldn't put it past him. She would have to figure out something that would prove to herself anyway, that he was the only thief around.

As she thought about it, a plan started in her mind. Somehow she would find something that would make a dark dye. Then she had to find a way to have it explode in his face for everyone to see. It had to be waterproof so he couldn't just wash it off. Now, what did she have, that fit that description?

She found an old package of dark blue powdered dye that Grampa evidently was going to use for something. She put it in a light weight plastic wrap, then in a heavier bag, to carry it to her trapline, in.

The next morning, she took 3 of the bigger traps that she had not treated, out on the trail. She set them in conspicuous spots along her trap line, then slightly camouflaged them. She didn't want them to look too easy to find. Then she bent a young sapling down and attached a trip line to it. She tied one of the baggies of dye to the sapling. If an animal tripped it, it would get a shower of blue dye but if a person tripped it, it was about face height. Hopefully, they would get a face full of blue powder. It would be hard to remove and should show up for some time. The trip line was hooked to the trap, so that anyone trying to move or tamper with the trap would get the dye. She had some pieces of fur scrap that she arranged in the trap, so from a distance it would look like something was in the trap. She did this with all 3 trap sites. Then she returned to the cabin.

Two days later, one of the traps had snowshoe

tracks around it and it had tripped. The person had
fell backwards when the sapling snapped forward
and from the looks of the snow, the dye had hit full
in the head. She picked up the rest of the traps and
removed the dye bombs. She was well pleased with
the day's work.

The next morning, she was surprised to hear a
couple of snow machines pull up in her yard. A
young man and woman were on one of the
machines and Bill was on the other one. Bill's face
was a ghastly bluish tinge that didn't look too
healthy. Jo couldn't help but smile at him. The
young man came over to her door, Jo stepped out,
with her shotgun down at her side. The young man
noticed it immediately and nodded. He said,
"Ma'am, I want to introduce myself and my wife.
We are Ned and Jody Long. We have a small
homestead a few miles up the road. This fellow has
been staying in our little cabin and had been paying
us rent, with small amounts of gold in the summer
and a few marten furs this winter. Yesterday, he
came back with blue dye all over him. I didn't think
much of him, anyway, but he could not explain how
he had gotten the stuff all over his face. We just
happened to see him coming in or we might not
have seen him at all until it wore off. Anyway, I
backtracked him and I saw you picking up your traps
and undoing your bombs. Then I followed you back
down to your cabin. I met your grandfather a few
years ago and he was a fine man. He always treated
me right and helped us through some bad spots in

our first couple of years. We don't hold with thievery and it looks to me like this man has been causing you problems all along. We were just going to take him to the village and turn him loose, unless you want to press charges. We will tell everyone there what he has been up to. They will not welcome him with open arms. We spent the gold but we still have the furs and have them here, for you. We feel responsible for letting him stay with us and letting him remain in the area by doing so. We are sorry and if you are ever up our way, please stop in. We would like to have your company."

Jo thanked him, but said she wouldn't press charges against Bill. Just living with himself would be sentence enough. She told them not to worry about the gold and to please keep the furs, if they could use them. She had only trapped a few for some things she wanted to make and had as many as she needed, now. She asked them to stop by, anytime, and visit.

As the young man walked back to the snow machine, Jo noticed that his wife had a pistol aimed in the general vicinity of Bill. She could not manage any sympathy for him. He brought it all on himself.

Ned and Jody stopped by the next day on their way back from the village. They brought her mail and stayed to talk a little while. They had told everyone at the Post Office about Bill and what he had been doing. They thought the girl he had been staying with in the river bank cabin had let him move back in with her. Jody was very shy and it took a while for her to feel comfortable enough too say very much. When she spotted the tiny cabin birdhouses though, she had to say something. Jo told her a friend had made them for her for Christmas, for the swallows. The cabins had Astroturf sod roofs and were made from dowels, notched and fitted together like logs. Will had taken a lot of time, making them. Jody wondered if he would mind if she made some like them, for sale to the tourist shops. Jo didn't know but told her she would ask, the next time she saw or wrote to Will.

Jo still had some of the Christmas candy frozen, in her back room so she sent some home with Ned and Jody in one of her birch bark baskets. She had made several baskets, trying to get them right. She still thought there was room for improvement.

It was nice to know there were some neighbors just a few miles away. Even if she didn't see them often, they were there and they seemed like nice people. It wasn't so much that they were anti-social, as just shy and reserved. She was surprised to learn that Jody was expecting their first child in a little over a month. She hadn't looked pregnant. But then, winter clothing hid a lot. Jo had gotten several more rabbits, the smaller Snowshoe hares, not the larger Arctic Hares. She saved all the skins and now thought she would make Jody's baby something Alaskan to wear.

She thought maybe a tiny parka and mukluks would do fine. She started softening the skins that evening for her new project. She thought the rest of the burgundy velvet would do for a lining, for the baby clothes.

Chapter 22

The winter seemed to be going by quite rapidly
and she still hadn't finished several of her projects.
She sketched Sitka, Atigun and Toolik laying in a
heap on her bed with the log wall behind them. The
sketch looked okay to her so now she was painting
it. Somehow the painting didn't resemble the sketch
all that much, but it was fun.

She was studying the small engine repair manual
and was practicing on the rototiller engine. She
hoped she would have it back together in good
order in time for spring planting. She didn't now
how early to plant, but would follow Grampa's
journals. She had read most of his journals from
the time he arrived in Alaska and had learned a lot
from them.

A couple of weeks later, while she was working on
the baby clothes, she heard a plane circling so went
outside. It was Steve's, so she started the pickup and
went down to pick him up. She had kept the airstrip
plowed of snow, at least most of it. There was a
packed snow base as the snowplow left a couple of
inches if snow under it. Steve's plane was on skis,
but she didn't know how deep of snow it could land

on. It had seemed like a good idea at the time, anyway.

The weather had warmed up quite a bit, it was sunny and the temperature was staying around zero. But in the sun, it felt quite warm. She guessed just about any rise in temperature would feel warm by comparison to the extreme cold of winter.

Steve had the oil drained from his plane when she arrived and he had several sacks of stuff in the plane for her. He had brought fresh fruit and some fresh vegetables and she really appreciated his thoughtfulness.

As they came through the door of the cabin, his eyes fell on the tiny little parka and mukluks she was working on, on the table. His face got white and he dropped the bag of groceries he was carrying. He grabbed Jo and pulled her to him.

"Why didn't you tell me? How soon is it due? Is it too late for an abortion? We'll get married, why didn't you <u>tell</u> me?"

Jo was so startled that it took a moment to figure out what he was even talking about. The only part that seemed to register was abortion.

"I don't believe in abortion, Steve.. I don't know what you are talking about, but I don't believe in abortion for me. I think that is each person's individual decision, but I know for me, I could not handle it."

"Were you ever going to let me know? Or were you going to be noble and have our baby by yourself?"

"Our baby? What are you talking about? I'm not having a baby."

Then her eyes followed the direction his were looking and saw the little clothes.

"Oh, those. I'm making them for Jody. Her baby is due in a little while and I wanted something Alaskan for her."

"Who's Jody?"

"She's Ned's wife. They're the homesteaders up on the hill.."

Jo proceeded to tell him about Bill and how she had met Ned and Jody. Steve was not happy about having Bill still in the area. He was worried about what the man might do to Jo. Bill seemed to blame all of his bad decisions on her. Like most people, Bill never took the blame, himself, for his own stupidity. Steve was rather relieved, though, that Jo was not pregnant. He didn't think he would make a very good father. It would certainly put an end to his swinging bachelor image, wouldn't it? He mentioned this to Jo and they laughed about his taking a baby with him on his dates.

Then she told him she had run out of birth control pills last month, so unless they wanted the joke to become the reality, they would have to cool it. He told her he was like the scouts, always prepared.

Jo unpacked the bags Steve had brought out. There were even fresh eggs. Hers were getting to have a distinct flavor and aroma that left a lot to be desired from an egg. The eggs kept quite well in the cellar, but they were not as good as fresh eggs. Steve had brought several dozen so they would last her quite a while.

There was about 8 ½ hours of sunlight a day now, so they had a lot of time to explore. She offered him the skis or the snowshoes. He chose the skis. Sitka was immediately ready to take him for a spin. So he hooked up the line and off they went. He had forgotten to ask Jo what the commands were, so just went along for the ride, wherever Sitka decided to take him.

They returned quite a while later, both out of breath. Sitka flopped down in the snow and Steve leaned against the cabin. He said he didn't realize how out of shape he was, but then, he had always preferred indoor sports and lunged for her. He had forgotten the skis and her snowshoes didn't help much either and they were soon a tangle of equipment and themselves on the ground. They got the gear untangled and back on their feet. That was about all the outdoors he could stand, he told her. So they put up the equipment and went back inside the cabin.

The next morning, Steve told her he had to fly to the village on business and would she like to come along? Of course she would. They were soon at the airplane and the warm oil poured back in. The takeoff was smooth and he told her it was nice, having the runway plowed. It was only a few minutes flight to the village and they landed a little bumpy, but okay.

Jo went to the Post Office and mailed her letters and picked up her mail. Then they went over to Harlan's cabin as he was the one Steve had to see. Jo asked directions to Thad's cabin and went on over to visit with him. While Steve and Harlan finished their business. She would come back in an hour.

Fanny was at Thad's place and they had a good visit. They were both glad to see her and find out that she was enjoying her winter. A lot of people can't take the winters in Alaska, too much cold and dark. Also, most didn't like being alone, like she was. That really made some people a little bit crazy.

Thad told several stories of cabin fever hitting people, some were funny, some were not. Partners sometimes did strange things from splitting everything they owned in half, to murder. Now the scientists were saying that a lot of it came from staying in a small air-tight cabin without getting out into the fresh air. The lack of fresh air affected their brain and also the lack of light.

Thad and Fanny walked back to Harlan's with her and everyone had a good visit. Harlan and Fanny fixed up a lunch for everyone and they stayed until Steven mentioned the lack of landing lights at her airstrip. Harlan and Thad told her they would be moving back to their cabins on the claims as soon as breakup started. They had just about all of town living they could stand. Jo told them about Bill and the Longs. Thad had been at the Post Office when they brought Bill in. He said they had not left anything out, even their letting Bill rent from them.

He thought they were pretty nice people. Bill was still living with the girl by the river. She was convinced he was going to marry her. She was always bragging about getting married to her rich lover. Jo wished her a lot of luck, she was going to need it.

Steve flew back to Fairbanks the next afternoon with the papers he had from Harlan. He said he would try to make it back out the next weekend, but couldn't promise. A lot depended on the weather and the road was closed now and would remain closed until the first of April. Then the road crew would have it open. Even though the sun was shining almost every day, the snow hadn't started melting yet.

As the days slowly warmed up, Jo noticed spots leaking in the cabin roof. It had not leaked at all in the summer with all the rain but now there were drips in unlikely places. She had to keep moving pans and kettles and buckets all around the cabin, trying to catch the drips. She cleared all the snow from the roof but could not see where any of it had melted. So what was all the water in the cabin? Where was it coming from and what could she do to remedy it? The drips continued for the next couple of weeks then stopped. She still did not know what was causing them. She mentioned this to Ned and Jody and they laughed.

"It sounds like frost buildup over the winter in your ceiling. There probably isn't a vapor barrier in that old cabin and when the frost started melting, it just dripped all over your cabin. You would have to shovel all the sod off the roof, put down a layer of visqueen, then put your sod back." Ned told her.

"So, what is visqueen?"

"Visqueen is just heavy plastic. It's used to wrap the inside of buildings with, for a vapor barrier to prevent the problem you've been having, with frost buildup in the walls and ceiling. It doesn't happen in log walls, but in frame houses, it can rot out the walls. It is a whole different way of building, up here. When your cabin was built, they didn't have the rolls of plastic to use. But now it can't be done without. We use it for everything around here."

Jo decided to fix her roof this summer. She didn't want to have to put pans all over the room every spring. Besides, the roof would be starting to rot from the moisture if it wasn't, already.

Jody was due to have her baby any time now and Jo was worried. They did not plan on going to town. They were planning a home birth. The baby was already dropped and turned, so they knew it would be very soon. Jo had delivered many calves and been around when the mares foaled, but a baby was a bit different, she thought. She wished them luck and decided to drop by every day, if she could.

Steve had not made it back out but had sent a message on the radio to let her know so she wouldn't be expecting him and worry. She had gotten several letters when they went to the village and a lot of catalogues. She had made out an order for vegetable seeds and had it ready when Steve left and he mailed it for her. So she should have a box of seeds waiting for her the next time she went for mail. She had made out her list during the winter, from entries in Grampa's journals so it hadn't taken long to make out the order forms in the catalogues, once she had them.

When she arrived at the Long's on Friday, Jody was in labor. She didn't know whether she should stay or if Jody would be more comfortable without her there. Ned and Jody both assured her they would welcome having her stay. Their confidence seemed to diminish as the actual birth drew closer.

Jo's presence seemed to reassure them even though she knew less about what was gong on than they did. They had studied several books and just before winter, had been in a class for expectant parents in Fairbanks. So Jo stayed and talked of everything she could think of to take their minds off the possible problems of birth.

The actual birth was very quick and surprised them all. The baby was a perfectly formed little girl and they were extremely pleased with her. Jo prepared some soup for Jody even though she wanted a steak and then went home. She would bring her present tomorrow.

Jo took her camera with her when she returned the next day. She thought maybe they would like a family portrait shot, to send to their families. They thought the parka and mukluks were adorable and dressed the baby in them for her portrait. Jody put on her parka also and had a picture taken of her and her daughter in their parkas. They had named the baby Melissa.

There had been lots of mail from the various government agencies with permit forms to be filled out for the upcoming mining season. Jo had filled them out to the best of her knowledge and returned them. She had not gotten anything back yet, so didn't know if her mining was going to be permitted this summer or not. It was aggravating trying to work with the agencies. Since her claims were patented, she did not have to fool with a lot of the paperwork that the other Miners had to do. She could not believe what some of the agencies required. Some of it was not even feasible.

There were Miners that were not responsible people and mined in a manner that was not suitable. But the few did not warrant the harsh regulations that had been made to regulate mining in the last several years. Most Miners were very conscious of the impact on the environment and worked to minimize it. These were mostly small family Miners that intended to work here the rest of their lives.

They did not want to look at ugly scenes so took care of it as they worked it. The original intent of the laws the regulations were loosely based on, were admirable. There should not be toxic chemicals released into the atmosphere or the water or soil. But family placer gold mining does not add any chemicals although now the agencies were trying to get the Miners to add chemicals to make the water artificially clear. Jo was afraid the added chemicals would have a long term affect on the environment. They had not been tested sufficiently for her to feel safe with using them. But many uninformed people only saw the clear water and thought that was aesthetically more pleasing so was all right. The fact that turbid water supplied food for fish and other aquatic life was not the issue. They just liked seeing lovely clear water.

By the middle of March, Jo heard on the radio that one of the Miners in her area was being cited for noncompliance by the EPA. The fine could be as high as $10,000 per offence per day. She did not know the people but they were not, as the news release put it, "Flagrant Violators." In fact, they had worked closely with some of the agencies trying to develop better technology. Their own records were being used as the evidence against them. It didn't seem fair to Jo.

Steve had not been back although his absence did not leave a void in her life. She did enjoy his company when he was here. She just was not in love with him so it didn't really matter whether he was there or not. She would always be thankful to him for showing her that she was not a frigid person and had a healthy appetite for enjoying a physical relationship. He was also a good friend. She hoped he would remain a friend. She thought the scare of her possible pregnancy had given him some second thoughts about continuing their present relationship in quite the same way.

One morning a few days later, she heard a plane

circle the cabin but it didn't sound like Steve's. When she went out to look, it was a smaller plane but it circled twice, waggled it's wings then headed for the airstrip.

She was surprised to see Will standing by the plane. He told her he was licensed now and wanted to get more flying time so thought he would stop by and see how she was, since he was in the area. He had a silly grin when he said that, so she suspected the area, loosely translated, meant when he left Fairbanks. She couldn't understand why she was so glad to see him.

For that matter, he wasn't sure why he had decided to come out here for the weekend. He was no longer working for the E.C.S. and they had not parted on particularly friendly terms, so what was he doing here? For that matter, why had he left Fairbanks before Lorraine got home? He knew she would have wanted to come with him. But it always seemed there were other people around, whenever he was with Jo and he wanted to be alone with her and get better acquainted. He had stopped and got some fresh produce to bring and some special foods for their dinner tonight. He wanted to cook for her, for a change. She always did things for him and for everyone else too.

As she drove back to the cabin, Jo could not figure out why she had such a fluttery feeling in her stomach and why she felt a little odd. It was a nice feeling, but odd.

There was still a lot of snow on the ground, but it

was melting a bit more every day. They spent the afternoon companionably working on her projects. There was 12 hours of sunlight per day now, and they had plenty of time to see what they were doing. It was nice, working with Will. He didn't automatically try to be the boss just because he was male. He worked with her on an equal basis.

They talked and found that they had a lot in common. They had a lot of the same philosophies on life and the same likes and dislikes on food and movies. They both enjoyed reading and doing things for themselves. Both preferred living out of town. They each wondered why they had not got along to start with.

Sitka was in 7th heaven when Will was around. They played and wrestled in the snow. Will found that the melting snow was hard and wet, not the light fluffy stuff of cold winter weather. Soon, his clothing was soaked through. Sitka flopped down on top of him and got him even wetter. A slight breeze started up and he was soon chilled to the bone.

He finally went to the cabin and changed his clothes, but still felt chilled. He fixed their dinner, that night. He had brought a couple of lobster tails, and broiled them while he prepared a salad and toasted garlic bread. He clarified some butter and added some seasonings to it to dip the lobster in. The meal turned out lovely and Jo thanked him for his thoughtfulness. She had a blueberry pie from the last of the fresh blueberries packed in sugar from the summer. So they had quite a feast.

Lorraine sent a message out, to both of them, referring to her brother, the rat, for leaving without her.

Will put his sleeping bag on the couch and they turned out the lights and prepared for bed. Jo awoke several hours later to hear Will tossing and turning. She put on a robe and went over to see what was the matter. He had a high fever and was muttering about freezing. She put a quilt over him, but it didn't seem to help. So she got him to move back to her bed. She piled the quilts over him then cuddled up next to his feverish body. She had given him some aspirin, but didn't know what else to do.

He was shivering so bad, she hoped that her body heat would help him. They both fell into a troubled sleep and she awoke in the morning, his fever had gone down and he was sleeping peacefully. She got up without waking him and got dressed. She would let him sleep as long as he could, it would help him feel better.

When he finally woke up, he was disoriented for a few seconds. How had he got here, in Jo's bed? Just what had he done last night? Where was Jo and had he done something she would never forgive him for? He had wanted to sleep with her for a long time, but he wanted to at least remember what happened, when he did.

Hs head ached and his mouth tasted horrible. His body felt like every bone had been improperly set and the muscles screamed every time he attempted to move. Just what <u>had</u> happened last night? He felt like warmed over death. He didn't remember drinking anything to make him feel like this.

Jo came in while he was contemplating all this and came over to the bed. She sat on the edge and felt his forehead. It felt normal and he seemed to be okay. He wouldn't look directly at her and mumbled a question at her. She had to get him to repeat it, before she could figure out what he was saying.

When it dawned on her that he was worried about what happened last night, she almost gave in to the impulse to make him really worry. But looking at his miserable expression stopped her. He was really worried, already. So she told him the truth. The relief on his face was plain to see and she was glad she hadn't teased him. But she couldn't help but tell him what she had almost said. He grabbed her and pulled her over onto the bed. He felt weak, but she wasn't putting up a struggle so he succeeded.

"What, you would make a sick person suffer even more, you heartless person? I had all sorts of images going through my mind, that you would hate me or that I had made a complete ass of myself or some other total mess of whatever I had done here, in your bed. I've wanted to be here for so long and then to not even remember what had happened, that really wiped me out. To think, I actually spent the night with you cuddled up against me and <u>nothing</u> happened is almost as bad. I don't now whether to be sorry, thinking I did, or be sorry that I didn't."

She had to laugh at his expression. He looked so

woebegone, that she reached over and kissed his cheek. He still had her halfway pinned down on the bed. He told her a kiss on the cheek did not make up for the mental anguish he had just gone through and kissed her on the mouth. They were both surprised at the immediate fire that ignited between them. He leaned back on his pillow and she got up from the bed.

They were both a bit subdued as she prepared something for breakfast. She did like Will, more than she was willing to admit, even to herself. She would have to think this over. She was not sorry for her fling with Steve, but it was over. She wasn't sorry it was over, either. She had learned a lot about herself and enjoyed being with Steve. He had never wanted their relationship to be more than casual and neither did she.

She supposed she should feel immoral, because of her attitude, but she didn't. It had seemed right at the time and was a lovely memory. So now she would get on with her life. After having this little talk with herself, she had everything sorted into it's proper place in her mind. Then she was back to being her usual cheerful self.

Will was not sure what to think. He wanted her, that much he knew, but how much he wanted her, surprised him. She seemed to have lodged somewhere next to his heart and would not budge. He could not say what it was about her that affected him so. He had tried his best, all winter, to get her out of his mind and feelings. He dated numerous women that fit his idea of his type of woman. None had rated a second date; He had done his best to forget Jo but all it did was more firmly entrench her in his thoughts. He loved being with her, she was bright, had a marvelous sense of humor, was capable of looking after herself and didn't take him seriously. That last thought really bothered him.

He had studied Resource Development and Marketing during his winter of partial unemployment. He had gotten a part time job working at the refinery. It had amazed him to realize the safeguards that were used to prevent ecological damage.

His environmental training must have been a bit out of date. They were still working on the assumption that all resource developers were ruining the world. Some probably are and worth going after. But the environmental groups were all for throwing out the baby with the bath water. They wanted everything stopped. He wondered how he could have been so blind. He had just been several years out of date.

Now he wondered how the radical groups expected to live, once they achieved their goals and shut down resource development. Return to the Stone Age? No, they couldn't even disturb the stones. It would have to be more primitive than that, even. No thanks. He wasn't ready to live like that.

What he would really like, was to live like Jo was.

Living from what he could do on his own. Work with his own hands and build his own environment. If he wanted to be lazy, he would just do without.

His standard of living would depend on his own work. He liked that idea. It was a little old-fashioned, too, but at least it was honest. After all, it was the original foundation for the country. He felt better after his little talk with himself. In fact, he felt like getting up and doing some work. Jo had other ideas, however, and he found that he was weaker than he had thought. He reluctantly ate breakfast in bed and thought he was fine. But as soon as he tried to sit on the edge of the bed, his head spun and he thought he would cover himself in glory and faint. He was certainly making a lot of points with Jo on this trip. Of course, he didn't think he had ever exactly come out looking good, in any of their encounters. So he gave in to Jo's insistence that he remain in bed and was a very rude invalid, most of the day.

Jo let him read from some of Grampa's journals and soon he was engrossed in them. They were such a wealth of knowledge and experience that he couldn't put them down. By the end of the day, he had learned more from reading those journals than he had during his first few years of college. He told Jo that she should consider making a book from these journals and publish it. Everyone should have the opportunity to read them.

When it was time for bed, Will offered to move back to the couch. Jo told him she would sleep there, since he was already comfortable, so why move. He graciously offered to share the bed but she declined, saying he was too sick to have to make such a sacrifice. He assured her that he was feeling fine and it would be no sacrifice.

She laughed and tossed a pillow at him. It was a large feather pillow and caught him off guard. It knocked him flat. He wasn't in as fine of shape as he thought he was, if a pillow could flatten him, she told him and went to bed on the couch.

He grumbled about not being taken seriously when his offer was in good faith. He even offered to fold the sheets so they wouldn't be touching. She still refused and told him to go to sleep. He would be glad she hadn't taken advantage of him, later. He seriously doubted that and told her so. They both laughed and went to sleep.

Chapter 23

He felt fine the next morning and insisted on getting up and doing for himself. After breakfast, they hung the birdhouses he gave her for Christmas in the trees around the cabin. She asked if Jody could use his idea for the birdhouses. He said he seriously doubted if he would ever make any more of them and she was welcome to them.

By lunch time, he was tired out so she convinced him he should rest on the bed for a while. He sleepily invited her to join him and was surprised when she did. He immediately fell asleep and was disappointed when he awoke to find her gone. She was out in the garden, clearing away some of the old debris that was showing up through the snow. Was he always going to fall asleep when he was near her? The thought depressed him. That's certainly not what he had in mind, and that's a fact.

She had put a light blanket over him when she got up and he felt like he was about 10 years old again. He didn't want to be mothered, he wanted an adult, loving relationship with her. But to him, it looked like wanting was all he was ever going to get. She was driving him up a wall and he didn't even know what to do about it. She seemed to enjoy his kisses and had not denied liking him, so what was he to do?

He got up and folded the blanket. He found a warm jacket hanging on a peg and went outdoors. He was feeling much better, and thought he would probably live.

Jo still had a lot of snow around the garden, but she was breaking off the old dry stalks and carrying them to the fence. She had quite a stack of them on the other side. She had worked up part of the garden last autumn before freeze up but couldn't bring herself to till under plants that were still producing. By the time the weather finally killed the plants, the ground was frozen too hard to till, so the dried remains still protruded above the graying snow that persisted in staying on the ground.

She didn't want Will to overdo it. In his present condition, he could have a relapse. So they spent the afternoon planning the upcoming summer. Jo told him that she planned on a trip to the village in the next few days to pick up her mail and get her seed order. She wanted to start a few plants indoors on the windowsill if she could convince Atigun an Toolik to stay off them. They loved soaking up the sun and would spread out on the windowsill and sleep all day.

Will offered to fly her down in the morning before he headed back to Fairbanks. He had to go back in a day or two as he was just on Spring Break from school. She accepted, she wasn't sure of the condition of the road yet anyway, and hadn't looked forward to driving it.

Will still wasn't too sure of what he was going to be doing this summer. He had applications in with several of the mining companies and it was possible that his refinery job would become full time. He wasn't sure just what line of work to pursue.

Jo didn't want Will to over exert himself, so when he offered to share the bed with her, she agreed on a strictly platonic level. He was surprised that she agreed at all. He wasn't sure of his ability to remain on a strictly platonic level though, so insisted that he remake the bed with the sheets folded in half, lengthwise. She told him she would take her chances. He went outside while she prepared for bed. He turned the gas light out when he came back in. He stubbed his toe on the way to the bed and cursed mildly under his breath. He carefully stayed on his side of the bed and resolved to never ever be this honorable again, it was killing him.

Good intentions be darned, he would take his chances and turned toward her. The moonlight through the window gave just enough light that he could see her sleeping peacefully. She was totally unaware that he was going to break his promise not to touch her. He watched her a moment, he just could not awaken her. He groaned and turned his back to her, he would just have to tough it out.

She opened one eye an looked at his back, smiled, and closed her eye. She was pretty sure he would not turn her way again tonight.

He slowly woke up, realizing his ear was being licked and nuzzled. Jo! The dear girl was letting him know she wanted him, too. He turned toward her, to discover Atigun sitting on her pillow, starting to purr. He rubbed his wet ear and growled at the cat. The cat smiled at him, he would swear the cat smiled. Why on earth had he given her the darn cat, anyway. At that moment, he didn't much like cats.

Jo came in the cabin and saw that he was awake. She started breakfast preparations and asked if he wanted breakfast in bed. He told her only under the condition that she be the main course, She declined and set the table.

He dressed, grumbling about her uncooperative attitude. She told him it was his punishment for even thinking about breaking his promise to her, last night.

Now, how did she now that? She <u>had</u> been awake. He grabbed her as she set their full plates on the table. "You wicked girl, how come I still like you so much?"

They both collapsed laughing onto the couch. She knew he was going to kiss her and wasn't sure just how much longer her will power was going to last. This weekend hadn't been easy on her either. So she started tickling him. He proved to be just as ticklish as Lorraine had said he was. He held up his hands in surrender and pointed to their cooling breakfast. Their truce held all through breakfast, but they were inclined to giggle each time their eyes met.

After breakfast, they decided to fly to the village

and then Will would fly on to Fairbanks. He actually should have been studying on this long break from school. Jo threatened to save the dishes for him to do the next time he came out. He started bagging them up in a sack and said he would make Lorraine do them for telling Jo about his being ticklish.

"Well, just this one time I'll let you off. After all, you are taking me in for my mail."

"Yes, but did you hear me say anything about bringing you home? Huh? Did you? I'm going to leave you stranded." He twirled an imaginary mustache and leered in his best villain imitation.

Their flight to the village was uneventful. Will proved to be a cautious and conscientious pilot. Jo felt safe, even though she had had doubts when they started. After all, he had only been flying a few months. He told her there were old pilots and there were bold pilots, but there were no old, bold pilots.

There was a considerable amount of mail waiting for her at the Post Office. Everything she had ordered had arrived. And the junk mail was pouring in. Thad's "town" cabin was near the airstrip and they thought they recognized the plane, so came over to see. Both the men were pleased to see them and said they would be out to their cabins in a few days. They had everything but the perishables loaded in the old Jeep. Thad had brought a moose steak from his winter cache for Jo to take home. She kissed his cheek and totally ruined his composure. Fresh meat would be a treat. Jo told them they were expected at her place for dinner their first night out.

Thad was worried his moose meat would spoil with the weather getting so warm during the days now. He was canning as much as he could for summer use at the cabin. He thought he might get a freezer next year, then he could keep meat during the summer, too. Now that he had electricity to his cabin in the village, he could do that.

Harlan started teasing Thad about getting soft in his old age. Thad grinned and agreed that he was.

After Will headed back to Fairbanks, Jo took the mail up to Ned and Jody. They hadn't been to the village since before the baby was born. Melissa was growing fast and her parents were extremely proud of her. She was very good natured and Jody points out, "Who wouldn't be, with two large willing slaves at her beck and call."

About a week later, Thad and Harlan came by, in the old Jeep. They said that the road was not in very good condition yet and advised waiting another week or two before driving to the village. They had brought her mail out and said they would be down about 6 o'clock for dinner. Thad had brought her a box of moose meat to can and hoped she could use it.

She started a canner full of meat cooking and started some hot rolls for dinner. She sliced some of the moose meat into thin strips and put it in a teriyaki marinade, then went looking for some willow branches to peel for skewers. Pineapple chunks, onion and slices of meat on a skewer should broil nicely, she thought. She still had some nice large onions in the cellar and some cans of chunk pineapple, too. A jar of mixed vegetables from last year's garden and a fudge pie should make a tasty meal.

While looking for the pineapple in the cellar, she noticed that the crock of blueberries packed in sugar was starting to bubble slightly so changed dessert to blueberry pie.

Thad and Harlan loved the dinner and were surprised that the meat was some that Thad had just given her, earlier in the day. They spent the evening telling stories of the winter's happenings in the village and of the old days. They told of the fellow staying at the roadhouse that decided he wanted to go bowling. The nearest bowling alley was 150 miles away so he gathered up all the used liquor bottles and set them at the end of the hallway, upstairs. He couldn't find a regular ball of any kind, so used a heavy chunk of wood with a piece of limb on it to hold on to, as a ball. It didn't roll at all, so he slid it down the hallway. Kind of a cross between bowling and curling. After a few practice slides, he really got going and the resulting crashes and breaking glass roused everyone still trying to sleep. Soon they had a tournament of sorts going. Regardless of the roadhouse owner's pleas, the tourney lasted until all available bottles were smashed. The next morning, complete with hangovers, the tourney participants got to clean the upstairs hallway.

Fanny had promised to marry both Harlan and

Thad and they were waiting to see how she would settle that one. They thought it would be a very long engagement. Jo doubted if any of them really wanted to get married.

Later, as Jo prepared for bed, she thought over the evening and was glad the fellows were back.

She had received some of the permits required for her to mine this summer, in the mail the men brought out for her. It didn't seem possible that the snow would actually be entirely gone in a few weeks and everything would be green and blooming. The arrival of Thad and Harlan marked the end of winter. She had learned a lot and survived with very little hardship. She knew that every winter would not be this easy. She had been lucky to have such good friends helping her along.

Jo had started some garden seeds in some soil she took from the cellar walls an placed in egg cartons. Atigun and Toolik did not take kindly to having their window sill taken over by these and Jo did not like finding them stretched out on top of the cartons, so she finally built a couple of shelves higher up on the inside of her windows. Now the seedlings were up in a few of the cartons. By March 21st, there was 12 hours of sunlight a day and the snow disappeared rapidly after that. Now her yard was a sea of mud. She was building a framework of poles to use as a mini-greenhouse at the front of the cabin. It would only be a temporary arrangement until she could manage something better near the garden. She covered the frame with a couple of layers of plastic and moved her egg cartons of seedlings out there during the day. It still was too cold at night, once in a while, to take the chance of leaving them out.

As she reread one of Grampa's notes from the bag of garden seeds he left in the cellar, it was almost like he were standing behind her, guiding her along.

'Now about the first or second week of April, I usually plant a couple of the rows in the garden that I hilled up last fall, before freeze-up. I know it looks like it is too early, but I always do. So far, I have never lost any of the plantings, either. Plant everything in little short rows, 2 or 3 across the top of each hilled row. There's some plastic gallon jugs with the bottoms cut out that I put over a few hills of squash and bean seeds. If you space these along the rows, it holds the plastic up and you have some little greenhouse rows. Plant a bit of everything and then you can transplant to the other rows, later. Put 2 or 3 layers of plastic over the whole works. After you uncover the rows during the day, you can remove the lids on the gallon jugs and replace at night when you recover the rows.'

She had followed his instructions but the ground seemed so cold and she didn't think anything would grow this year. There was still snow in the hollows between the rows. It would never work.

The soil had warmed up enough in her little frame by the cabin that she transplanted some of the seedlings directly into the soil. She was surprised to see small seedlings coming up in the covered rows of the garden. The plastic usually had so much condensation on it that she couldn't be sure whether the green was weeds or some of the stuff she planted.

Atigun and Toolik wanted to be outside during the day, now, but she was afraid to let them wander. There were a pair of large owls nesting nearby and she had seen eagles in the area, also. Some good sized hawks circled around once in a while plus some of the animals in the area wouldn't mind adding cats to their menu. So she put them in the roofed pen she and Lorraine had built, last summer. They soon tolerated it and didn't complain too much.

Sitka had developed into a lovely dog. He still thought he was a puppy and would try to snuggle onto her lap when he wanted attention. She made some saddlebags for him and he carried their lunch when they went exploring. He was big enough now that it was usually too warm in the cabin for very long, for his comfort. So at night, he was put in the shed on the back of the cabin and during the day, he roamed loose in the yard around the cabin. The cats stayed in the cabin most of the time, except their daily time in the pen in good weather while Jo worked in the yard or garden. Thad asked her what their sentence was, life?

The geese flew north over the cabin in huge flocks, honking and gabbling. Their flight seemed to mark the true beginning of spring. The buds were swelling on the trees and she had tried tapping some of the birches earlier, for syrup. She knew she didn't have it figured out quite yet. The syrup was good, but she only got about a pint. It takes 90 gallons of birch sap to make 1 gallon of syrup. She would have to do something different next year.

The amount of steam that boiled off clouded her windows and left the cabin smelling syrupy. It would be better to set up outdoors to do it. Maybe even in the shop. Now why didn't she think of that before? She could have used the barrel stove. Oh well, hind sight is always 20/20.

She greased and cleaned on the old dozer and went over the pump, as well. She wanted to be sure that everything was in perfect working order. Taking good care of it would be a lot easier than having to replace something later if she neglected it.

Chapter 24

The ice was going out on the large rivers and she listened to the progress of breakup on the radio. Most of the villages were built near the rivers as the rivers supplied everything needed to live.

But in the spring, the ice going out was treacherous. Blocks as large as a house would be tossed into the air as though they were foam. Jams of ice could dam the river flow and water would back up far above the river banks. The grinding ice pulverized anything in it's path leaving chaos in it's wake.

The bears were out of hibernation and in very foul humor. She had seen one roll out of a snow bank, earlier, then sit there like a pouty child, rubbing it's eyes with large clumsy appearing paws. He had plopped over on his side and napped with his head on his paws. She had carefully backed away and left him sleeping. The clumsy appearance was deceiving and she did not want to be the first thing a hungry bear noticed upon awakening. Luckily, she had Sitka on a leash that day and he never barked.

Bill was missing and presumed dead! She found it hard to believe, but all the evidence pointed to his death. He had been drinking heavily for some time and the girl he was living with was about fed up with him. He had started staying late at the roadhouse, drinking morosely in a corner by himself.

He came home late one night, as the ice was going out, and started an argument with the girl. They argued some and he began knocking her around. She grabbed a stick of firewood and belted him a good one, he backed to the door with her hitting him all the way. They did not hear the river ice just beyond her yard and when Bill ran outside, he disappeared into a swirl of ice and water that was rising around her cabin. The river channel was undercutting the bank and left her cabin perched precariously on the new edge of the river. No body had been found, but in the conditions, that was not surprising.

Jo could not say she would miss him, but it was a shame for anyone to die that way. She wrote and told her family about it. She knew they would feel sorry for him. They still found it hard to believe what he was really like.

The garden astounded her. She had never seen anything grow as fast as the tiny seedlings were doing. The covered rows in the garden were outdoing the things she started indoors, earlier. The shock of being transplanted must have made the difference, she guessed.

The trees were leafing out so fast she could notice

the difference in the size of the leaves from day to day. Spring had lasted 2 weeks. Now it was summer. Thad told her there were two seasons in the Interior of Alaska, winter and mosquitoes. This was definitely mosquitoes. They were large and lethargic, but still bit with great capacity. It was time to start using the Alaskan perfume, bug repellant.

The road was open to Fairbanks now and Thad and Harlan decided they needed a holiday in 'Sin City' before the start of the summer's work. They invited Jo and she readily accepted. It would be nice to go to town.

They decided to go to Fairbanks on a Thursday evening, so they would have a business day, Friday, to take care of anything necessary. Then Saturday would be for fun and come back to the mines Sunday morning.

The old car was washed and serviced, in top shape for their trip. Of course the muddy road to town would make sure it didn't look that good when they got there. Jo helped and promised to pack a fine lunch to snack on. She made some meat pies with a bread dough crust. The filling was spicy and very good. They were still warm from the oven when Thad and Harlan pulled up in the car. Snack time started immediately and they enjoyed the fresh cut onions from Jo's perennial onion bed behind the cabin.

A bear with tiny twin cubs were sunning themselves on a hillside near the road. The cubs tumbled over each other and played like puppies. Jo was glad they were many miles from her cabin. They were darling to watch, but a mother bear is very dangerous.

A bit farther, a cow moose with twin calves crossed the road in front of them. Harlan and Thad agreed that the bear would probably have one or both calves before the end of the summer.

When they reached the paved highway, Jo was surprised at the amount of road affected by frost heaves. The pavement was broken in places with dips and dives where there had been fairly decent road the summer before.

They checked in at the same place they had stayed the summer before. All had friends in town, but they didn't want anyone to feel obligated to house, feed and entertain them. After they got settled in their rooms, they made plans to meet in the lobby. They would decide where to go for dinner and what they wanted to do for the evening.

The hot bath felt heavenly to Jo. It had been a long time since she had enjoyed a bath this much. No pumping the water, no heating it on the stove. The well was a blessing, but it was still work to have a bath. She was almost surprised that her hair dryer still worked. She fastened her hair back with fancy combs and finished her makeup. She never had used very much and thought it best not to overdo it. She decided a dress was in order after the long winter of jeans, insulated pants and parkas.

Harlan and Thad both whistled as she walked into the lobby of the hotel. They were both profuse with their compliments and escorted her to the car. As least her ego wouldn't suffer from listening to them. In fact, if she took them seriously, she might get an over inflated one.

A new restaurant had opened and the clerk at the hotel praised the food and service. They decided to try it out. The décor was lovely, the lighting subdued without needing a flashlight to read the menu. The food was delicious. Of course everyone agreed any meal not cooked by yourself after a long winter tended to be that way.

After dinner, they went to a movie, agreeing that since none of them had seen any movies, there was bound to be one they had not seen, playing somewhere. There was and they enjoyed themselves, stuffing down popcorn and soda as though they had not just eaten a large meal a short time before. Groaning, they made their way to the car, then the hotel.

It wasn't very late when Jo got to her room so she decided to call Lorraine and see if she would like to spend the day with Jo tomorrow. Lorraine was delighted to hear that Jo was in town. She was free and would love to spend the day running around on errands with Jo. She had lots of news, too much to tell on the phone.

Will came in as Lorraine hung up the phone. "Who was that at this time of day?" he asked.

Lorraine smiled and said, "You'll see, tomorrow. Plan on being here for dinner. We are having guests."

Lorraine was waiting in the lobby the next morning when Jo came down. She explained that she was just too excited to keep quiet around Will and wanted to surprise him by having them be there for dinner when he got home from work.

"Oh please, you have to come over for dinner. All of you have been so nice to me. I want to fix something for you, for a change. Please?"

Harlan and Thad could never turn down a plea from a lady and Jo didn't, either. Of course, when Lorraine dropped to her knees while batting her eyelashes, begging, in the lobby with everyone staring at them, she couldn't have refused. Laughing, they helped Lorraine to her feet and half carried her out to the car to join them for breakfast.

The day passed swiftly with visits to several government agencies to confirm last minute details before the mining season started. Most of the shopping for supplies was completed also. Perishable items would be purchased just before leaving town to return to their cabins. Jo purchased several rolls of heavy plastic for her roof. She planned on fixing it before the mining season got started. She had been doing preparatory work for the last 2 weeks, but until the thick ice melted around her sluice box and dam, she could not totally set up for work. It amazed her that such a small stream could build solid ice 15 to 20 feet thick up the entire valley. It overflowed and froze, then overflowed and repeated the process the entire winter. Glaciering was what the local people called it. She thought she might attempt to fix an ice house this summer and cut ice for it, next winter. She asked Harlan and Thad about it and if they could recommend materials she might need. She purchased nails and hinges and thought she would have enough extra plastic from her roofing project to build a small icehouse. It would be nice to have, during the summer.

Lorraine asked to be dropped at her place so she could prepare dinner. She asked that they arrive a little before Will was due home from work. She wanted to have everything ready when he came in.

The surprise party turned out to be more of a surprise than even Lorraine had anticipated. As Will parked his car and started for the house, a taxi pulled up out front. A girl with several pieces of luggage paid the driver and started purposefully toward the door. As she neared, Lorraine groaned. "Oh no, not Miriam. I thought we had seen the last of her 2 years ago. Will will be absolutely furious. She is bound and determined to marry him."

As a distraught Will and a triumphant looking Miriam came through the door, Jo couldn't help giggling a little. Will' eyes flew to her in a mute appeal for help. Jo's eyes seemed to answer 'anything for a friend'.

Jo sauntered over to Will, placed her arms around his neck, kissed him slowly and thoroughly and asked him who his little friend was. Miriam had gone from red to white and back to red, through this. Will, striving for composure and more than happy for the unexpected help, introduced everyone.

Once started, Jo couldn't seem to give up the role and languidly speculated on the possible sleeping arrangements for the night, as Miriam seemed prepared to stay an extended length of time. With a 2 bedroom apartment and 6 people, her combinations were varied and hilarious.

Thad did nothing to discourage her and entered into the speculations, then Lorraine mentioned that Mike was going to be there soon, too. No one mentioned that Jo, Harlan and Thad had rooms at the hotel or that Mike had his own place. Miriam was sure that everyone actually was staying there and that she was expected to sleep with everyone except Will. Jo managed to never pair the two of them, in any of her speculations. Aghast, Miriam spotted the phone and quickly placed a call for a taxi. She wouldn't even stay inside while waiting for it to appear. But stood out by her pile of luggage.

Lorraine couldn't keep still any longer and laughed so hard she thought she would never stop. Gulping through her laughter, she tried to explain who Miriam was. Mike had arrived by the back door and Lorraine was explaining the whole thing to him, also. Finally Will got a word in edgewise and made some sense from Lorraine's giggling tale.

Miriam's family lived near Will and Lorraine's family back in their home town. She was a spoiled only child and her family was very well to do., they indulged her every whim. She decided she wanted Will while they were still in high school. At first he had been flattered, she was beautiful and popular. But when she told him they would get married right after graduation and he would go to work for her father, Will rebelled.

By then he was totally disillusioned by her tantrums and sulks. She had been furious when he refused. She immediately married another fellow and made his life miserable until he divorced her. She remarried, divorced and remarried again within a couple of years. Evidently, she thought absence would have made Will's heart grow fonder of her that prompted this trip north. Maybe she even thought he would welcome her rescue of him from the Frozen North. Maybe now she thought he was a "Rich Alaskan" although money was not one of her worries.

Chapter 25

Lorraine's giggles were stopped by a faint wisp of smoke drifting in from the kitchen. With a wail, she ran to the kitchen, to return with a pan full of charred mystery meal. Her woebegone face looked on the verge of tears. No one could bring themselves to tease her. She had wanted to show her skills as cook and make a nice thank you dinner for everyone.

It was decided to celebrate the absence of Miriam by going out to dinner. In her case, absence definitely was making several hearts grow fonder. Especially Will's for Jo. They carried on their game through the evening, with Jo playing the clinging vine. It was difficult as they were about the same height, but she managed.

She was wearing the new dress her sister sent for Christmas. It was not one she would have picked out for herself, but after trying it on, she decided maybe her sister should pick out all her clothes. Her hair was braided in small braids pulled away from her face with the rest rippling free down her back. It shimmered in the lights and Will could hardly keep his eyes off her. He could not decide what it was about her that drew him to her so.

From the restaurant, they went to a night spot that had a good band and spent the rest of the evening visiting and dancing. There was a whole winter's worth of news to catch up on. Thad had a slightly jaundiced view of his family and old home area he had visited during the winter. His view on paved farms lost nothing in the telling.

Everyone was interested in Jo's winter. When she told them she didn't have time to be lonely, there was open skepticism. So she told them her schedule, get up, care for pets, fix breakfast, study until daylight, which took longer each day until December 21st. Then as the days lengthened, study until noon. Run her small trapline, pack wood to keep her supply in the cabin filled, skin any animals caught, fix dinner for herself and pets, do the day's dishes, put a large container of water on the barrel stove to heat, listen for messages at the allotted time on the radio, read or sketch for an hour or two, bathe, stoke the fire and go to bed.

There were also propane bottles to change, when one ran empty, the one for the stove didn't last as long as the one for her lights. Snow to shovel if it snowed. She periodically started the barrel stove in the shop to heat the old truck. She wanted it to start if she should have need to leave in a hurry. She had worked on the rototiller motor and was almost overwhelmed when it started again, after she put it back together and on the tiller.

As soon as the ground thawed enough, the garden

was started and now was showing signs of the long daylight hours in it's amazing growth. Her narrow escape from bad frostbite had made her much more careful in her explorations.

Taking a shortcut one day, she had gone through an overflow on the little stream by the cabin. The shock of the icy water had taken her breath away. Luckily, it was a small stream and the open water under the thin shell of ice fairly shallow. Snow concealed the thinness of the ice and she was in water over her knees before she knew it. The temperature was -36 degrees, F. and she knew the danger. Running up the hill to the cabin took only a few minutes but the ice forming on her legs and boots made it feel like forever.

Her mitts were frozen to the sleeves of her parka, but she was afraid she would burn herself if she got too close to the stove. She beat her mitts together, stomped her feet and finally, the ice cracked enough to pull the mitts off. She quickly worked her boots loose, then stripped, shivering, and stood in a tub while pouring water over herself. Then she sat down in the warm water and soaked. The pain of returning circulation was almost unbearable. She had only a couple of large blisters that healed quite soon to remind her of the possibility of such an accident being fatal. If it happened farther from warmth, if she were unable to start a fire, any number of if's.

She did not have time to get bored. With all the new things she was learning, there wasn't time to indulge in foolishness. She thought she might make several trappers hats next winter to sell to the tourist shops in town. As soon as she qualified for a resident hunting/fishing/trapping license, she would purchase one. Then she could trap furs and sell the finished products.

They teased her a bit about her plans for the next winter, when this one was barely over. Most people plan summer to summer, in a climate like this one. They knew she had decided to stay in Alaska.

Lorraine was taking several classes at the University and working a part time job. She and Mike had decided to get married as soon as they could afford a down payment on a house near town. They both liked the Bush, but not enough to contemplate living there in the winter, also.

Mike was taking classes at the University also. He had joined one of the Unions and planned to work on the north Slope during the winter and mine during the summer. They would soon have their home.

Will enjoyed his job at the small refinery and was taking night courses in related subjects. He now possessed a pilot's license, which he was proud of. He wasn't sure what he was going to do next.

Harlan figured he was satisfied with the things he was doing and reckoned to continue doing them.

Thad said he wasn't about to go back "Outside" again. It made a fellow plumb nervous just watching everyone rushing around not really doing anything that he could tell. He would join Harlan, mine in the summer, hunt and fish in the autumn, visit with the other people in the village during the winter, play some cards and rehash old times, do some ice fishing and plan the next mining season. Repair equipment in the spring, lay out the ground to be worked, it did take up a fellow's time. He couldn't think of a better life.

Saturday night seemed to turn into Sunday morning. Thad and Harlan said they wanted at least a couple of hours sleep before heading back to the creeks. Jo agreed, so the party broke up.

Will never did get a chance to talk to Jo, except the times they danced together. That had not been satisfactory, as there were always other people close enough to overhear what was being said. His mind was in a turmoil, this whole experience was something he could have done without. Not only was his life's work altered to a whole new field, his view of women had undergone a drastic overhaul, also.

After a not-very-early start, they stopped at a grocery store and bought fresh perishable items. The old Caddy was very well loaded for their return trip. As they neared the turn-off for the road to their claims, an old car careened toward them, narrowly missing the Cadillac as it spun on by. The driver was hunched down in the seat with a hat pulled low over his forehead. None of them could see who it was and no one recognized the car. Harlan did get the license number and make of the car written down. They would certainly mention this to the State Trooper that occasionally passed this way.

A thin column of smoke drew their attention towards Jo's place. There should not be any smoke. Thad speeded up and as they sped around the corner, Jo's heart fell. The small shed attached to the back of the cabin was in flames. Thad parked the car well back and Jo found her house keys. She had the front door unlocked in a second and the animals raced out of the cabin. The smoke curled under the door from the shed.

Harlan had tried to start her dozer, but didn't know her safeguards to get it started. He ran into the cabin, grabbed Jo. He quickly explained the possibility of saving the cabin itself if the shed were pushed away. Jo sincerely hoped so. The old dozer started immediately and she came in from the side, pushing the burning shed away from the main cabin. Thad and Harlan beat at the flames with blankets grabbed from her bed. The fire on the cabin itself was soon extinguished, but the shed and contents were a total loss. The back door was almost charred through. The smell of diesel was strong in the air. The fire was deliberately set. But why?

As reaction to the fire set in, Jo found that her legs refused to further support her. She sank to the ground and covered her face with her hands. If they had stayed in town a little longer, everything would have been lost. Sitka, Atigun and Toolik would have died. Grampa's treasures would have burned. If she had been here, what would have happened?

Would she now be in the ruins of the burned cabin, the victim of an accident? She was sure it was supposed to look like an accident. The smell of diesel probably would have dissipated before anyone happened by. Once again, her vulnerability was driven home with a vengeance. Any person living alone is more vulnerable than if there is another person to share the experience with.

Harlan stayed with Jo while Thad drove to the village to phone the description of the car and the license number to the Troopers. There were not many roads and if they started looking now, the possibility of catching the car were good.

Enough smoke had entered the cabin to coat everything in a black oily film. Jo and Harlan started cleaning, as soon as she recovered a bit. Why? It kept going around in her brain. Why would anyone do this?

They packed as much stuff as possible out in the yard. Then started scrubbing the ceiling logs, then the walls. They pumped gallons of water and started soaking her clothes. Almost all her winter clothes had been in the shed. She would have to replace them before winter. Much of the stuff was of more sentimental value than actual, but it could never be replaced. The special things that had been Grampa's. It was like losing him again.

The animals were reluctant to re-enter the cabin. The smell of smoke still clung to everything. Jo got her sleeping bag from the shop and placed it on the mattress on the bed. The sheets and blankets were soaking in a tub of water in the yard. She wasn't sure they would ever be usable again. The blanket she always put on the couch for the animals to sleep on when she was gone, saved the couch from being smoky but it had the odor. Thad and Harlan said they would take turns staying nights in the bunkhouse out back. One would be back later to spend the night. No one mentioned the possibility of the person responsible for the fire returning to finish what had been started, but it was in the back of each one's mind. The shotgun that hung over the door was thoroughly cleaned of smoke and well oiled. Jo's pistol had been between the mattress and box spring, so wasn't smoky. She would keep it handy from now on.

As Jo went to bed, the animals all piled on the bed with her. They needed reassurance, also, and she knew they would be alert to anyone outside, so she let them stay on the bed. Sitka was full grown now and a lovely large dog. He would be a good protector and was large enough to intimidate an intruder.

When Harlan returned a while later, the animals raised their heads and listened for a while, but recognized his sounds and settled back to sleep.

A few hours later, Sitka started growling deep in his throat. Atigun and Toolik joined him and Jo crawled from her sleeping bag to find out what the problem was. She pulled on her jeans and a T-shirt, before stepping outdoors. The shotgun still had the rifled slug in it for bears, but she wasn't sure what had awakened them. Sitka caught a scent and took off at a run to the other side of the shop. Jo and Harlan ran to the shop, Sitka had a man cornered against the building.

As he turned toward them, Jo gasped in surprise. Bill Humphries. Impossible. He was dead. By the look on Harlan's face, he soon would be, again. As Harlan raised his gun, Jo placed a hand on his shoulder.

"No, we just can't. Then we would be reduced to his level of person. I know no one would ever know, but we still have to live with ourselves."

"I know, but it's just so darn tempting. We'd be doing the world a favor by wiping out some vermin."

Harlan started looking for some rope to tie him up with, when Jo got the idea to let Bill do some of the cleanup work. He muttered and complained but was soon scrubbing heavy blankets on a washboard in a tub of soapy water in the yard. Every time he slowed down, Jo would fire the shotgun to spray near his feet. Occasionally a stray pellet would hit him and he would scream. Harlan thought it would probably have been kinder to shoot him outright. Jo said she didn't think he was suffering any permanent damage. She had replaced the lead shot with rock salt, it would dissolve away, with quite a bit of pain. If anyone deserved a bit of pain, she thought it was Bill. Harlan told her she had a slightly warped outlook on Bill. She agreed.

After Bill had washed the blankets, sheets and

most of the other items needing cleaned, Jo relented enough to prepare something for everyone to eat. As they ate, she asked Bill how he survived the fall into the river ice. After a brief sullen silence, he started talking.

When the water closed over him, he thought he was a goner, but a large piece of ice lifted him high above the water and tossed him far up on the bank of the river. Another piece of ice, about the size of a house almost crushed him but he managed to roll aside with only minor injuries. He managed to get to the roadhouse without anyone seeing him. George Watson was staying there and gave him a change of clothes. He slipped out the back way while George was checking out and having breakfast the next morning. George got a lunch to take with him and Bill ate it as they drove to Fairbanks. George let him stay at his place near Fairbanks. It wouldn't hurt to let everyone think he was dead and the fellow he had sold the claims to would quit looking for him. He would not admit he tried to burn the cabin, but the 5 gallons of diesel he had dropped when Sitka cornered him certainly looked suspicious.

Thad stopped by and decided that since everyone thought Bill was dead, already, they should either keep him as a slave or go ahead and kill him again. How could a person get in trouble for killing a dead man? Harlan solemnly agreed. Jo wasn't sure if they were joking or serious. Neither was Bill. He broke down and confessed to the whole thing. Thad said Bill wouldn't have made a very good slave anyway, his clothes washing wasn't quite up to snuff. The whites weren't sparkling white and the colors didn't gleam.

While Bill was staying with George, they had decided to force Jo out. George blamed her for the loss of his job and a lot of money he had personally spent on the project. Bill figured she was the cause of all his problems, too. George strongly hinted that the old man's death was not an accident. He would occasionally gloat about the perfect crime, while they were drinking together.

Harlan went to the village to call the Troopers. Thad stayed to help Jo and keep an eye on Bill. The three of them worked until Harlan got back an hour or so later. The Troopers would be out in 2 or 3 hours to pick up Bill. They packed the bed and couch outdoors to air and proceeded to rewash the entire inside of the cabin. Harlan had picked up some more cleaning supplies in the village and with 4 people working, albeit one wasn't too willing, the smell of smoke was soon replaced with the smell of pine cleaner. They were scraping the charred logs on the back of the cabin when the Troopers arrived.

Bill immediately clammed up and denied everything as soon as the Trooper read him his Rights. Thad smiled sweetly, agreed Bill should keep quiet, the Troopers wouldn't take him and Bill would be left to their tender mercies. Bill opened up like a floodgate. He told the Troopers more than they could possibly want to know about anything and everything he had ever been involved in, in his whole life. Things no one ever suspected he was even remotely involved in. The police in Oregon would be mighty interested in a lot of things he was spilling. One of the Troopers told them it was a good thing they had read him his Rights before he started spouting off or they would not have been able to record his confession. They would pick up George Watson as soon as they got to Fairbanks.

Chapter 26

Jo felt dazed by the recent events. She loved living here, she knew she would never be rich. But she could live comfortably all her life, right here. Most of her food could be grown or harvested here. But Bill had made her realize her vulnerability. The weather and wild animals could be coped with. They may be unpredictable, but still, as long as a person is prepared and watchful, not necessarily life threatening.

People could not be depended on to react in any prescribed manner. At one time, she was seriously intending on marrying Bill and now she didn't care whether he lived or died. How could she trust her feelings toward any man? She knew she had never been in love with Steve, She knew it at the time when they were involved with each other. He had given her much to cherish. Mike had been a brief fantasy, but never one that she took seriously. Will did not fit any of the niches. She knew her feelings for him were different than any she had ever felt before. But did he feel the same? He seemed so happy to see her, yet also ill at ease in her presence.

The few times they had kissed still brought tingles to her, just thinking about them. Maybe it was another case of lust.

The next day, Jo went through all the washed items. Some were fine but others would only be fit to use as rags. Her small wardrobe couldn't take much more weeding out. The sheets and light towels still had a dull look to them so she decided to use the rest of the dye she had used as a bomb during the winter.

She built a fire outdoors under a wash tub, hauled water out and added the sheets and towels. After the mixture heated up, she mixed the dye and poured it into the tub. A long stick served to stir the mess. She rinsed them in the creek, to ensure plenty of fresh water. Everything would be navy blue, but it wouldn't be dingy.

The sound of a helicopter coming in low woke Jo the next morning. She hurriedly dressed as it landed in the road near the cabin. A Trooper stepped down an came to the door.

"Miss Akins? I have some property that belongs to you. While searching George Watson's property, yesterday afternoon, some correspondence was found that was intended for you but apparently never reached you. We have made copies for you as the originals must be kept as evidence. Tampering with the U.S. mail now makes this a Federal case. May I look around and take some pictures?"

Jo explained that they had done a lot of cleaning up. She had taken some pictures, herself, while they were cleaning, but didn't now if that would help. He assured her that they would help. Then she finished the roll and gave him the film to develop. She really needed to get a new digital camera, film and developing was getting hard to find.   He would return the negatives and unrelated photos to her.

There were geological reports in the papers the Trooper brought her. The studies made by the company George Watson once represented showed some commercial quality veins of gold with silver, running 1 ounce gold and 2 ½ ounces of silver to the ton. There was a request for permission to determine the quantity available to mine. The colored stones Jo occasionally found were mostly garnet with a few poor quality diamonds. Mostly a curiosity rather than of economic value.

The other letters were requests to hear from her. Evidently George and Bill were keeping track of her incoming and outgoing mail somehow.

Jo wrote a quick note to the mining company explaining the delay in her responding and letting them know she was not interested. If she changed her mind in the future, she would let them be the first to know.

The Trooper finished his investigation and took the letters she wanted mailed with him, back to Fairbanks.

The rest of the week seemed to fly by, with fixing her things as much as possible back in the cabin and trying to get ready to mine. The garden needed weeding almost every day. If she let more than a couple of days go by, the weeds seemed to outgrow everything else. The vegetables were doing their fair share of growing, also. The 24 hours of light per day really triggers plant growth. Some of the plants went to seed immediately, though. Some types of radishes, turnips, lettuce and chard seemed to seed almost as soon as they grew through the ground. Other types of the same varieties grew fine and large. The fresh salads were appreciated after the long winter of canned and dried foods. Lambs Quarters and Strawberry Spinach were gathered as fresh greens, then pulled as weeds, from the garden. Everything fresh tasted good.

Somehow, Jo was not surprised to see Will pull up in front of the cabin, late Friday evening. She was starting to dig the sod loose from the roof of the cabin as he drove up. He offered to come up and help, but she could tell that he was tired. He must have left Fairbanks directly after getting off work. Somehow, she had lost track of time and realized she was tired and hungry, too. She quickly covered the roof with plastic, weighted down with a few strategically placed rocks and came down.

As she stepped from the ladder, Will's arms closed around her and he kissed her, softly, tenderly but with much feeling.

"Oh, Jo, I've been so worried about you. After I read about Bill in the paper and your fire, I had to come. I was going to, anyway, but not tonight."

"You know you are always welcome. You don't need to have an excuse to visit me."

"I know. I just feel like I'm imposing, what with you letting Lorraine stay with you last summer and all. I really wish you would stay with us, when you are in town."

"I've usually been with someone, whenever I've gone to Fairbanks and it seemed easier to stay together. But I do thank you and if I go in alone, I'll certainly accept your offer. Would you like something to eat? I'm starving."

Will kept his arm around her as they went into the cabin. He had been so worried that maybe she was hurt, or something. She was so special and didn't even realize it.

He remembered the groceries, after they got inside, but was loath to let go of her. He wheeled them both around and they went to his pickup, together. If he had his way, she wouldn't get any further away from him than she was, right now.

His hello kiss had started familiar tingles inside Jo. She didn't know what to expect from him, but she knew she didn't want this time to end like all their other times together seemed to. If she had anything to do about it, he would be beside her. The rest of the weekend, anyway. She fixed a marinade for the steaks, while he scrubbed a couple of baking potatoes. After placing the potatoes in the oven, they went to the garden and picked enough trimmings for a fresh salad. They worked in companionable silence, each seeming to know what needed done, without words. Just before the potatoes were done, she placed the steaks in the broiler. They set the table, fixed the salad and seemed to drift into small kisses as they worked.

She excused herself for a quick shower before eating. As she stepped under the cool spray, Will stepped into the shower house, "Do you need your back scrubbed?" he asked innocently.

She considered the question a whole 2 seconds before saying yes. After all, she couldn't rush and let him know she wanted him, could she?

He yelped when he stepped under the cool water. He didn't know until then that there was no heat, except the sun hitting the tank. At this time of day, it didn't. This was going just like all his plans in the past. He wanted a nice long leisurely shower, to wash her whole body, and was getting a cold shower instead. He should have known.

She turned him away from her and started soaping his back and he started forgetting the cold water. Her slippery front barely touched his back, as she reached his neck and shoulders. She laughed and lightly slapped his bare bottom, telling him it was his turn to wash her back. The water felt wonderful, as he soaped her back, starting at her neck and working his way to her feet. Somehow his hands seemed to have a life of their own and were also soaping her front. She felt so good. As she turned to face him, the water felt positively warm. Her hands were doing marvelous things with soap.

"What about dinner?"

"What about it?"

"It's going to burn."

"I turned the stove off before I followed you out here."

"Ummmm."

Without bothering to dress, they went back into the cabin, kissing and touching all the way. Will stretched her out on the bed, worshipping her with his eyes as he lay down beside her. His fingers gently skimmed over her damp body, followed by light kisses. She reciprocated, touching, kissing, until they were both almost beyond control. They both wanted to savor this time together. Will pulled away from her to use protection, before they joined.

Jo thought she had experienced the ultimate in sensual enjoyment, but found that she didn't know as much as she thought she did. Actually having feelings for Will added a new dimension to the pleasure. She was afraid to admit she loved Will. Instead, she rationalized that it had been so long since she had done this, that any attractive, thoughtful lover would be able to affect her this way. But he did make her feel soooo good all over.

Will always considered himself rather a connoisseur of making love. This was beyond any experience he had ever engaged in. She was a marvelous lover. If this was what it was like, making love to girls that were not his type, then he was missing out on the best he ever had. He was more than a little afraid that this was not going to get her out of his system. Already, he wanted her again.

He ran his fingertips over her body, just feather light touches, almost too light to feel, but incredibly arousing. She could feel his hardness against her and the magic of his fingers and lips aroused her even more. Soon she could stand it no longer and started working her own magic on him.

Total exhaustion finally brought them back to thoughts of dinner. It was overdone and only slightly warm, but they ate it with relish and enjoyed every bite. Cleanup took only minutes and then they were back on the bed.

The rest of the night was spent making love, sleeping, waking and making love again. It was the most energetic night either had ever spent, yet they both felt refreshed in the morning. Both had some muscle twinges and tender spots, but felt marvelous. Will was determined to have her out of his system by Sunday night and Jo would not admit she loved him, either, but both were drawn to each other like magnets. Most of the weekend was spent like the first night.

Sunday evening, Will prepared to leave. He had to be at work early Monday morning or he wouldn't have left. He felt bereft as he left her. Dang, he still didn't have her out of his system. What on earth would it take? He didn't think he could live with her or without her.

After the second time he said goodbye, the first time was interrupted by another lust attack, Jo went back into the cabin. For the first time ever, it seemed lonely without someone sharing it with her. No, not someone, Will. It was lonely without Will.

Could she trust her feelings? He never mentioned

love or wanting to share more than the passing moment with her. What were his feelings toward her? Was she making yet another mistake with a man? They had gone from open antagonism to truce to friendship. Was love another step in their relationship? Memories of the weekend brought a smile to her face. That man could certainly love with his body, if not with his mind. If nothing else, this trip to Alaska had certainly opened her eyes to a lot of things she had been missing out on.

Her self esteem was raised to the point her family would consider her conceited, possibly. She had always been self reliant, but now she knew she could survive under conditions most people would consider primitive, and enjoy it. She now knew she could appreciate a physical relationship without feeling guilty or ashamed. Yes, she had certainly learned a lot in Alaska. No wonder she loved it here.

The next morning, she started work on the roof again. The good weather would not last forever and she didn't want the roof in worse condition than it already was. She decided to work on half at a time. Then she wouldn't have to throw the dirt off the roof, then hoist it back up on the roof, later. Under the layer of dirt, she found birch bark, laid like shingles. It shed the rain and didn't rot. She left it in place, spreading the plastic over it. Then she placed a layer of foam board over the plastic and another layer of plastic. Then a layer of cardboard and newspapers to keep small stones from puncturing the plastic. She shoveled a few inches of the dry dirt over the paper and placed yet another layer of plastic, then the rest of the dirt. The sod was rolled back on top, a little worse for wear. She would haul water up and water it well if it didn't rain in the next day or two.

The layer of dry dirt might help insulate just a little bit better in the winter. She would have liked to use a lot of thick foam board, but just couldn't afford it and had not had a way to haul it out on any of her trips. Dirt isn't the best insulating material, but it is free and takes a long time for cold to penetrate, or heat either, for that matter. That's why log cabins feel so warm in winter and cool in the summer.

By the end of the week, most of the roof work was done. The ice was melting slowly from her sluicing area. It seemed impossible for ice to melt so slowly with the weather so hot. No wonder the pond had been so cold when she first tried swimming in it last summer. The ice must have barely left the pond.

The roof of the cabin was low and Grampa had banked dirt up around the lower logs of the cabin, itself, so Jo leaned the ladder up like a stair step to get on the roof. She packed buckets of water up to water the replaced sod. Sitka ran up and down the ladder as a new game. Jo was pouring the last bucket of water on the roof when Sitka growled and pressed against her legs.

Following his gaze, she saw a small black bear

meandering toward the cabin. There was not time to get into the cabin, from up there, she just hoped she could pull the ladder up with her on the roof before the bear reached it.

Fear adds strength she found. The ladder came up easily and she hastily scrambled back to the highest peak of the cabin roof. Sitka leaned against her as she sat watching the bear.

It was actually not a very big bear, maybe on it's own for the first time. It wandered around the cabin, occasionally standing on it's hind legs and peering at her on the roof. It wandered over near the woodpile, sat down flat on it's rump with it's legs sticking out straight in front of it. It cocked it's head from side to side, as though trying to figure out why she was sitting there and why the dog kept growling, low in it's throat.

She knew it looked harmless and that she had lost her initial fear of it. But even a bear that size could attack and maul or kill a person. They were actually more dangerous because without their mothers for the first time, they were usually starving.

Bears are very unpredictable and can act one way and suddenly change into a totally different acting animal. She started to put the ladder down, at the back of the cabin, but the bear immediately came around to the back. If she moved to the front, it did the same.

She sat down, the bear did, too. Maybe if she sat still, it would lose interest?

She sat up with a start, how long had she slept?

The sun was farther along it's summer arc, she must have slept at least an hour or so. Was the bear still here? She looked around the cabin and didn't spot it anywhere. She quickly put the ladder down and she and Sitka scrambled down, put the ladder flat on the ground and went into the cabin. The bear must have thought she was dull to watch once she fell asleep and wandered off in boredom. She would have to remember that. If she ever had an unwelcome guest.

Chapter 27

It had taken a bit more than a week to complete the work on the cabin roof. The garden definitely showed the lack of weeding, but at least the plants were all big enough, she could find them even with the prolific weeds. She got back on her schedule of so many hours preparing her mining site, so many hours in the garden and still study an hour or two. Her artwork was progressing quite well, she thought. As long as it pleased her, it didn't matter what anyone else thought of it. She would need to build another shed or room to replace the one that had burned, but that would have to wait. She thought about building another room of logs, so started looking for suitable trees to fall. Maybe by autumn, they would be dry enough to use, especially if she also peeled them now.

She wanted to try making items to sell in the gift shops in Fairbanks, during the winter and an extra room would be handy not only for storage but as a workroom.

She found enough trees on her own ground to build the addition with.. She had thought she might have to apply for a permit to get some house logs and was glad not to have to. She used the dozer to pull the logs down near the shop. She cut poles to lay them on, so air could circulate and dry them faster after she peeled them.

By the time she had the logs stacked, the ice was gone from her pond and she started sluicing every day. The regulations had changed yet again and now the fine for water quality violations was a possible $25,000.00 per day. Jo built huge earthen dams from old tailings, to contain and filter her waste water. Even though her creek had no fish, went a couple of miles then sank in a bog and never entered another stream, she still had to have drinking water quality at the end of her workings. No one used her stream below her, but none of that matters to government regulation makers. Their own regulations allowed variances and waivers to be granted on an individual basis, but no one ever received one, no matter what the circumstances. Since her stream was so small, she used all of the water and had no by-passes. All the water entered her settling ponds, to filter through the gravel of the old tailings. One person could make a living doing it this way, but a family would be hard pressed to survive. Soon, only the large mining companies would be able to afford to mine. The small family operators could not afford the regulation changes every year. If she wanted to live in town in the winter, she would have to get a job to support herself. The mining paid for the essentials to live out in the Bush, with enough for some luxuries, but not enough for living in town part of the year. Maybe, with the pump running this year, she would make more money.

Now that she recirculated the water, she could mine 4 hours per day, before the water got too muddy to wash the gold or go through the pump. She continued the practice of cleaning the upper riffles after every day's sluicing. There was no use taking chances and the first gold missing from her box last year was before Bill got here, so someone else had pilfered, too. It may have been someone passing through, she certainly hoped so. She didn't want to think that any of her neighbors might steal from her.

Mike and his father were mining now. Thad and Harlan were sluicing on their claims but neither wanted to overwork, so didn't do too much. One or the other usually stopped over to see how she was doing, every other night or so. Other than that, she had no company for almost a month. She missed Will and could not decide whether she was mad because he didn't come out, or relieved.

When Will did finally show up, he couldn't have picked a worse day, if he had sat down and tried. She forgot to refuel the pump, so it ran out. She couldn't get it restarted and ran the battery down. She came back to the shop and the manual wasn't where it was supposed to be, they had forgot to return it to it's place after using it repairing the pump last autumn. She finally found it under some parts, in a corner. Then the wrench slipped as she was bleeding the fuel lines and smashed 3 fingers. The three fingers were swollen and bloody and when she reached for the handhold on the dozer, she slipped from not getting a good grip. She fell and twisted her ankle and banged up her knee. She finally made it back to the cabin and was sitting, soaking her ankle, feeling sorry for herself, when <u>he</u> came waltzing in, as though he had only left yesterday.

"What do you want," she snarled.

Will stopped as though she had hit him. Whatever was wrong with Jo? She was always in a good mood. That was one of the things he loved about her. After much soul searching, he finally admitted to himself that indeed, he did love her.

He applied for a grant last winter to study reclaimed mining areas and the impact on local wildlife and just received notice it had been approved. This would give him a chance to live out here, with Jo. So why wasn't she happy to see him?

Only then did he notice the soaking ankle, the wrapped knuckles and the swollen knee.

"Good grief, Jo, what happened to you? Did someone attack you? Are you all right? Let me take you to a doctor."

Somewhat mollified by his belated concern, she explained her day to him. As she told it, it did sound funny, but that didn't stop her from throwing the pan of water on him when he laughed. Since the water was ice cold, it did stop his laughter. He sputtered and coughed while she glared at him.

Well, maybe she wasn't always in a good mood. As he thought of their first meeting, he recalled that she was seldom in a good mood. But he loved her anyway. He proceeded to tell her so as her mouth fell slowly open.

Here she had snarled at him, threw ice water on him and he was telling her that he loved her? Was she going about this love thing all wrong? She thought kindness, loving ways and thoughtfulness were the way to show love. He gently placed a finger under her chin and closed her mouth, then just as gently, he kissed her.

Love. Will loved her. Just when she had about convinced herself that she didn't even like him all that much, he went and did something like that.

As Jo sat in stunned silence, Will attempted to explain his absence and to apologize to her. She was still trying to assimilate that he actually had told her that he loved her. She started with a jerk when he waved his hand near her face.

"Will to Jo, Will to Jo, are you there, Jo?"

"But Will, if you think you love me, why haven't I heard from you since you were here, last? They still accept messages on the radio and if your arm was broken, I'm sure Lorraine or someone would have written a short note for you."

"Dear Love, you haven't heard a word that I have been saying. Plus, I don't "think" I love you, I <u>do</u> love you. When I was here last time, we had something very special together. It scared the hell out of me. I hate to think I'm a coward, but the longer I kept putting off talking to you or seeing you, the harder it became to actually do it. My job ended at the refinery a couple of days after I returned to town."

"I haven't been able to find a job. Lorraine keeps telling me what kind of idiot I am. I wish she would marry Mike and leave me alone, even though she is right. Then I just couldn't come out here and sponge off you. I've spent more sleepless nights than I care to think about, trying to analyze my feelings for you. It's impossible to neatly compartmentalize feelings, especially love. I know I am only happy when I am with you and that I would do anything in my power to make you happy, too. I have fought against it from the start, but I still love you. I thought I could get you out of my system, once we made love, that didn't work, resoundingly. I want you more than ever. I know this is sudden, but I want us to get married and eventually have a family."

"I'm sure you think you mean everything you just said, but I don't think it's love. I like you very much and I'll even admit I miss you while you were gone. But I don't know about loving you."

Will couldn't hide the sudden hurt in his eyes. He didn't want to even think about the possibility that Jo didn't believe him. Was nothing to ever work out as he planned? He sat, suddenly, on the couch. His whole being felt numb.

"May I stay here while I conduct my study? I can pay for my room and board. I should have waited, to tell you I love you, but to see you injured, while here by yourself, drove all sensible thoughts from my mind. I'm sorry if I made a fool out of myself. I'll try not to do that again. You know how I feel, so if you ever decide maybe you love me, too, just let me know."

Even in her grouchy-feel-sorry-for-herself state, Jo knew she had hurt his feelings rather badly. She didn't want to hurt him, but she wasn't sure of her ability to judge her own feelings. She had made a mess of things with Bill and still wasn't sure of her feelings for Will. He was special to her and she proceeded to tell him so. She tried to explain how she felt and why. He said he understood, but she could tell he thought she was trying to ease his feelings. He said as much and then she got mad.

"Will, I never have nor do I intend to ever, ease your mind by saying something I don't mean or feel. If you think back over our past encounters, you should know I have never tread lightly on your feelings nor anyone else's. I'm not about to start now. Yes, you can stay here, in the bunkhouse. We can work out some sort of arrangement later. I really am glad to see you. I think we should give ourselves time to really get better acquainted. We have known each other a bit over a year, but we haven't worked around each other nor have we been much more than 'company' when we have been together. Marriage is forever, to me."

Even though she made good sense, Will was not happy. He wanted everything to be worked out <u>now</u>, not in some dim future time. At least he would be near her every day. Maybe she would realize that she did love him, after all. Living in the bunkhouse wasn't exactly what he wanted, either, but it was better than not staying at all.

After he got his gear unpacked in the little bunkhouse, he came over to see if he could help Jo finish up her chores for the day. She had made her daily 'splash' even after hurting herself, so she only needed to work in her garden, yet today.

He offered to till between the rows and rake the sides of the raised rows as he hadn't a clue on what was good plants in the rows, themselves. That would at least make the garden look good. He could pack water to the garden, also. She hobbled out to keep him company and keep an eye on how he was doing in her garden. It wasn't that she didn't trust him to do a good job, but he had even admitted he didn't now what the good plants were and which were weeds.

He insisted on packing a chair out so she could at least be comfortable and then a bench to keep her swollen ankle and knee elevated.

By the time he had the garden tilled and raked the sides of the rows, he was tired and she was in much better spirits. They went back into the cabin in much better humor than when they came out, earlier.

She reheated some leftovers she had in her cellar for their dinner. The cellar stayed very cool year around, not freezing, but not warm, either. It made a perfect fridge. He asked if she could put the perishables he had brought out from town in her cellar as his ice chest wouldn't keep them cold for very long without a source of ice. He could go chop ice in some of the creeks farther up the road, but if she didn't mind, the cellar would work fine and he wanted her to use the food he brought out, anyway, for their meals.

After dinner, he washed the dishes, since she had fixed the meal. Then they played cribbage a while and talked a bit while they played. Soon they were back to their easy companionship. By the time he went to the little bunkhouse, he kissed her on the forehead and wished her goodnight. They were both feeling better about being here, together.

Harlan showed up just after noon, the next day and was surprised to see Will come out of the bunkhouse. He was really surprised when Will told him about the study he was doing about mine reclamation and impact. Harlan offered to show him several of the sites from the old days that had been shops and large camps. Thad knew where even more of them were located, over on the other side of the little Pass between this valley and the one north of it.

Will asked if he could record their talks about it all and take pictures to compare with the old time photos, and try to find the same angle and place to take his 'now' shots from to go with the 'before' photos.

Harlan thought it was about time someone did a

study like this. He thought Will should compile enough material to publish a book about the whole thing, also. Between the photos he and Thad had and if Jo would share some from her Grampa's collection, they could do a really good large book. Jo thought it was a great idea, later, when they discussed it after she got back from her daily splash and cleanup.

Thad even had some photos taken before any mining was done in some areas, then the mining pictures and they could get the 'now' photos at any time. The hills in the background would be the same in them all, to set the place for each.

Jo had all the reports from Fish & Game on fish production and also from Division of Mines on mineral production for him to use their own charts side by side for comparison.

Between Will's study and research and Jo's daily routine, they didn't see a lot of each other until evenings.

They would sit and discuss their day and how things were going. Each had suggestions for the other and found they liked working jointly on parts of the projects. Will had a laptop he plugged into his pickup lighter to charge and taught Jo how to use it. He was writing his report on the laptop and Jo was surprised to note he was giving her, Harlan and Thad credit for assistance. His second file was amazing. He had a digital camera and was loading all the photos taken at each site onto the laptop and scanned all the old photos with a handheld scanner he could use with the laptop, also. He kept the before and after photos together and it would be a beautiful informative book once he had it completed.

She found that they worked very well together. She enjoyed his company in the small everyday chores and jobs needing done to keep their life simple and enjoyable.

She was coming to realize she really had never known how to handle a relationship. It wasn't about the excitement of physical attraction although that was nice, but about mutual respect and caring for each other before there was anything physical about it. Not a popular point of view in today's world, but still the best way to start a lasting forever type of relationship.

One day as she approached her sluice box, she heard voices, so slid her shotgun into her arms for a quick response time in having it handy and walked quietly over the small rise to her sluice box. She had Will's digital camera with her and snapped a couple of pictures of the men riffling through her sluice box.

Two men were sitting at the head of her box, running their fingers through her riffles, checking for color.

"Find anything you like, yet?" She asked.

The men just about fell over themselves trying to stand up.

"Uh, we were just looking." One said.

"Yes, I can see that by the water dripping off your

hand and the gravel on top the riffles. Care to explain just why you think you have the right to steal from me?"

"Now just a minute there, we aren't thieves, we just wanted to look."

"Why is that any different than if I looked in your billfolds here or your bank accounts in town?" She asked.

"Why that would be illegal."

"Yes, and what you are doing is illegal, also. This is my livelihood and you are stealing it from me." She replied.

One of the men started to raise his fist toward her when the other one noticed the shotgun held loosely just under her arm. Her arm was coming up with the shotgun as his buddy was grabbing him from behind. When his eyes fell on the shotgun now pointed directly at his middle, he almost fainted.

"Look, I don't know what you think you are doing here, but if I ever catch you here again, I won't even fire a warning shot. Most of the Miners take a very dim view of thieves and you need to pay attention to private property." She told them.

One just needed to get the last word in and started in about public lands and all the resources belonging to the people.

She told them to put their hands on their heads and walk ahead of her to her cabin. They complained the entire walk down the hill. Will was coming out of the bunkhouse on a break when they reached the clearing. She asked him if he would get their billfolds and take down their personal information so she could turn it over to the Troopers and also take their picture with his digital camera to keep with the ID info. She handed him his camera and mentioned having taken their pictures while they were riffling her sluice box.

They started to complain and she told them they could do it alive or she could get the info off their bodies after she shot them, take their choice. Will suggested they comply as she had not had many good days lately and they really didn't want to see her get mad.

Will asked them if the pickup parked over on the side road was theirs and one said yes, it was. He told them he already had the information on it to give the Troopers and by the way they were parked, it looked like they had done this before.

One of the men still didn't see where they had done anything wrong and said yes, they did this every time they came out this road. It paid for their trip. The other one was kicking his leg, trying to get him to shut up.

Mike walked up the road as Jo was trying to decide what to do with them now. He recognized the men and wanted to punch them a few times. He and his dad had run them out of their workings last year. He offered to take them in to the Troopers if Jo would like. That would probably be the only thing that would teach them a lesson. The one was still blustering about the people's resources.

While Jo, Will and Mike discussed it, the two men

started easing away and Jo pulled the trigger on the shotgun aimed near their feet. Will and Mike jumped almost as high as the two men did.

"Sheesh, let a guy know ahead of time, will ya?" Mike said.

"Sorry, just wanted to get their attention." Jo answered.

Thad and Harlan pulled up in the old Jeep and asked who the two bear bait samples were. They had seen them before, also. Seems they had been sniping out of people's boxes out here for several years. This time they were caught red handed. One still had the sample bottle in his pocket. Every creek has a recognizable gold for that stream and once the gold in the bottle was analyzed, they would know for sure where it came from.

Will needed to turn in part of his report, Mike just wanted to take them in, Thad and Harlan also volunteered to escort them to town, so Jo asked if she could stay home. The guys said since she was the one that caught them with their hands in her sluice box, she would need to be the one filing the report.

They separated the men and made one drive their pickup while Harlan rode with him under cover of his handgun. Mike drove in the lead with the other one in his pickup, Thad sat with his handgun in his lap, aimed at the passenger. Will and Jo followed in Will's pickup. They didn't want the men to have an excuse to come back out for their pickup.

The Troopers seemed to know the two men as

they called them by name as they came through the door into their office. Jo told them how she caught the men and said one still had the vial of gold in his shirt pocket. She said she took their picture while they were still going through her sluicebox, which made the Trooper happy. He borrowed the memory card from Will's camera and got the pictures of the men off it.

They left the men in custody and decided to go out for dinner on their way home.

Chapter 28

They stopped at a popular truck stop along the highway on their way home. Dinner was delicious. Jo felt sure this answered her question about who was stealing from her before Bill showed up. It was a relief to know it was not one of her neighbors.

Jo fell asleep leaning against Will as he drove them home. Thad asked Will what his intentions were toward her. Will told him that as soon as he could convince her, he wanted to marry her. Thad said okay, that was sure a lot better than that Bill fellow she used to be engaged to, anyway, even if Will had started off on the wrong foot, he saw the error of his ways and was shaping up nicely.

Will wasn't sure, but thought he might have been slightly insulted but then approved of, so it was alright, no matter what. Both the old men were very protective of Jo and only wanted what was best for her. He could understand that, he just thought he was what was best for her. Now all he had to do was convince her of that.

Jo wasn't quite asleep while the men were talking, but figured after she heard what they were saying that she better keep on acting asleep. Just the fact that Will would discuss it with Thad was surprising. He seemed so sincere that she could not doubt he believed what he was saying. Soon, she really was deeply asleep.

When they reached her cabin, she was embarrassed to find she now was sleeping on Thad's shoulder. She felt so sorry for his poor arm. She was not a featherweight and he was not a large man. He patted her shoulder and said he could always have woke her up or pushed her back over onto Will if she had been too heavy. Besides, she only turned his way a mile or so back on the road when they made the turn off the main road and it wasn't often he got to have a pretty lady sleep against him. Then he blushed as he realized what he had just said.

Harlan came over from Mike's pickup and Mike turned and went home. The old Jeep was in front of her cabin, so the men got in and headed home. Will walked her to her door, kissed her cheek and went over to the little bunkhouse. It had been a long day.

The next day, when Will came out of the bunkhouse, he was a bit preoccupied and did not see the little bear cub run under the porch. The sow did see Will between her and her cub. She smacked him and he fell across the porch into the side of the bunkhouse with a yell. Jo heard the yell and came around the corner as the cub came back out from under the porch and saw the sow and cub take off into the woods.

Then she saw Will, crumpled against the bunkhouse and her heart skipped a few beats. She ran over to him, calling to him. He did not move. As she came closer, she saw blood. Now she was in a panic. What to do? She felt his neck and found a pulse, but there was a lot of blood. She tried to find where he was bleeding and saw a claw mark across his shoulder. As she pressed her hand against the mark, blood welled between her fingers and she felt light headed. She knew she had to help him and could not give in to faintness now. She held her head down a couple of minutes, then pulled off her T-shirt and pressed it tightly to the wound. There didn't appear to be any other injuries to him that she could find, other than the bump on his head from hitting the bunkhouse.

He moaned and she tried to straighten him out a bit better without reopening the shoulder wound. He finally opened his eyes and as they found focus, he relaxed when he found that she was holding the shirt to his shoulder. She asked if he could hold it with some pressure while she went and got supplies. He said he thought he could, but to watch for the bears. She told him they took off after he yelled and the cub came out from under the porch.

She put on another shirt in the cabin while looking for the first aid kit and more clean towels. He was still sitting up when she got back to him, but looking a little green around the edges. She helped him stand and held a lot of his weight as they made it over to the cabin. He was not looking good at all by the time they got inside. The bleeding had stopped and she cleaned the wound as well as she could. She made him pour the antiseptic over it, as she knew it would hurt badly. He poured and screamed at the same time, but he did get the wound covered very well. He even managed to jump and curse a little bit while doing it.

She closed the wound as well as she could and used butterfly bandages along the tear to hold it closed. He would have a scar from it, as she didn't think she could bring herself to sew him up. She doubted if he would hold still for that, either.

She settled him on the couch and brought him a large glass of water to drink and keep him hydrated. She knew that could be a problem and he would heal faster if he was well hydrated. She gave him some OTC painkillers and hoped they would stave off any fever, also. Bear claws are not the cleanest ways to get cut open and infection could be a real problem.

She stayed working around the cabin and immediate yard all afternoon, keeping an eye on him and keeping plenty of fluids handy for him to drink. The wound looked slightly swollen and red around it when she checked it later in the day. She bathed it in antiseptic and added some herbs to the water she rinsed it with.

When Harlan and Thad stopped by later on their way to the village, she asked them to see if the health aide had any antibiotics to send out for him. Ointment or pills, either one. She didn't want to make him ride the bumpy trip to see the health aide, but if they would not send anything out, he might have to go in.

When they came back a couple of hours later with the mail, they had a tube of ointment and a bottle of pills, both, for her to use. She was glad to see the medication as Will was starting to show signs of some fever and the edges of the wound were getting angry looking. She kept giving him the OTC painkillers and after he started on the antibiotic pills, everything seemed to look a bit better or she thought it did, anyway.

During the night, he woke her up, muttering in his sleep and she checked his forehead. He had a slight fever, so she woke him up enough to take some more OTC painkiller and another antibiotic.

By morning, he seemed to be over the worst of it or she hoped he was, anyway. She was a nervous wreck. At some point during the night, she realized he was the most important person in her life and the most important that had ever been in her life. She did not want to think of her life without him in it, in the future.

She fell asleep dreaming of telling him she actually did love him.

The next day was her usual day to go do the baking for the roadhouse in the village, but she didn't want to leave Will. He was feeling fairly good when he first woke up, so she helped him get cleaned up and dressed in clean clothes and he would ride to the village with her and let the health aide check him out in person.

By the time they reached the village, he wasn't feeling as good. So they went over to the health aide's cabin first. She checked him all over and said she couldn't have done any better and the butterfly bandages were doing a good job as long as he didn't pull them loose. The wound was clean and didn't look too inflamed since they started using the ointment on it and he was taking the pills. She gave them a few more pills and another tube of ointment.

Will curled up on the seat of the pickup and dozed off while Jo did the baking at the roadhouse. Things were still slow so she was only coming in once a week to bake. Once the tourists and fishermen, then later, hunters started coming in, the roadhouse would be much busier. They had sold all the pies she had made last trip, so asked if she could make a few more, this trip.

Jo mixed up the bread dough and set it for the first rising, then started the pies. She had mixed a huge amount of the dry ingredients for pie crust her first day on the job so now all she needed to do was dip out a cup of mix for each crust and add some cold water, mix just enough to hold together and roll out. While crusts were baking for cream pies, she filled other crusts with filling and added top crusts and soon had the ovens all filled and baking.

After punching down the bread dough for a 2nd rising, she checked on Will. He was still asleep, so she went back to her baking. She made cream fillings for the baked pie shells and filled them.

Coconut cream and chocolate cream were the two favorites, so she made extras. The filled pies were coming out of the oven as she shaped loaves and dinner rolls from the bread dough and included a pan of large cinnamon rolls.

The cream pies cooling in the walk-in fridge were cool enough to add the whipped topping, so she piled them high and set the fruit pies on the counter to cool.

The owner of the roadhouse came in and offered her a full time job as cook, but she had to refuse. She still mined in the summer and didn't want to give that up.

The bread products were ready to bake so she put them all in the ovens and again checked on Will. He was dozing, but opened his eyes as she looked in the window. She asked if he would like to come in and get something to eat. He needed another pill and shouldn't have it on an empty stomach. She helped him in and found a comfortable chair in the sitting room area. Then brought him a bowl of the day's soup and his pill.

As soon as all the breads were done, she helped Will back to the pickup and they headed back to the cabin. She settled him in the cabin and went up to make her daily splash.

By evening, he was running a bit of fever again. She bathed his shoulder with tepid water and some more of the OTC pain relievers. The wound looked a bit inflamed, but not too bad. She coated it well with the ointment.

During the night, he started thrashing around and muttering in his sleep. She sat on a cushion on the floor by the couch and held his hand and talked to him. Her voice seemed to quiet him down, so she sat there most of the night, and fell asleep sometime either very late or very early. She was still asleep leaning into the couch when someone banged on the door. Jo was disoriented and Will was still not too aware, so she finally got her robe tied better and went over to see who was banging on her door this early in the day.

A State Trooper stood there, looking stern and official. When he caught a glimpse of the ragged wound on Will's shoulder, his jaw dropped a bit. Jo invited him in and started a pot of hot water on the stove for some tea. Will started muttering and tossing around a bit and almost fell off the couch. The Trooper caught him and offered to move him over to the bed if she wanted.

She figured he better stay on the couch. She grabbed some clothes from yesterday and went back to the outhouse to get dressed. When she came in, the Trooper was seated by Will on a chair and looking at his shoulder. She told him what had happened and that the health aide had checked it and given them some antibiotics for it. Now he just needed time.

The Trooper finally got around to his reason for being here. The fellows they had brought in wanted to bring counter suit against her for having them arrested. She told the Trooper if she ever saw them around her sluice box or property again, she would just bury them and forget about doing the legal thing. He suggested she didn't really just tell him that, that she really would only harm them if they were inside her cabin and threatening her. She said the one had started toward her with his fist raised and she considered that a threat. He agreed that it was.

Now it came down to her word against theirs. She asked about the photos she had taken of them going through her sluice box. They claimed that was not at her property it was on a friend of theirs. So she took the Trooper up and showed him the little marks only on her sluice box that were some welding art she had practiced on, with the welder and dd they think they would ever find that on any other sluice box? Those marks showed in the photos.

They had admitted stealing from her although they didn't consider it stealing, for the last 2 years. At the current price of gold, she figured the men owed her quite a bit of money. If she figured it the way the various agencies figured how to assess fines, she would go by the amount of days they might have been doing it and charge so much per day. That ought to open their eyes a bit. The Trooper said he would try that and get back to her.

After making her splash and weeding in her garden a while, she painted up some warning signs to post around her property. Since this was patented property, it was the same as private property anywhere, and could be posted. Her signs left no doubt as to the penalty for trespassing.

Will slept most of the day, but it was finally a restful undisturbed type of sleep and she figured maybe he was on the mend. She fixed a pot of soup for dinner and started putting up some of her signs around her property.

When Harlan and Thad stopped by that evening, they had a few comments about her signs. So she told them about the Trooper and the fellows bringing counter-suit against her.

"Sure makes a person want to call in the Law, doesn't it?" asked Thad.

Everyone agreed. Will was sitting up on the couch, but still had a blanket over his lower body. His shoulder looked better, no redness to it at all, this evening. He asked Harlan and Thad to help him get back over to his bunkhouse and they obliged him.

Jo couldn't believe it, she missed him. Missed having him on the couch so she could check on him during the night. She even argued with herself about going over during the night to check on him. If he was asleep, she would wake him up and if he wasn't asleep, he might get the wrong idea.

She woke up crying during the night. She had just dreamed that Will died from the bear attack. She imagined her life without him in it and it stretched barren and alone ahead of her. She loved him. No matter if she fought against it, she loved the man, irritating as he could be.

When Will made his way back over to her cabin in the morning, she had a nice breakfast ready. They talked while they ate and finally Jo asked Will how he finally decided he loved her. He said it wasn't easy. He just knew that she was not his type, which brought a sputter of laughter from Jo. When he looked quizzically at her, she explained he was not her type, either, or that is what she had told herself all this past year.

He smiled at that and continued. "Pretty much I finally figured it out when it became obvious to me that I couldn't stand not being around you even if it is only as a friend. I would far rather it be more than as a friend, but if that is all you are willing to share with me, I will manage. It's my problem, not yours."

She thought back to how they worked together, and how well they managed to compliment each other's skills on projects they did, together. Even preparing a meal, they worked as a team on it. He was the only one of her group of friends that she truly missed, when he wasn't there. She enjoyed everyone's company, but if they were not around, it was no big deal.

Will thought he could do some work on his research on the laptop, in the bunkhouse, so slowly walked back over, refusing assistance.

While Jo was cleaning up in the cabin, Grampa's Bible fell open to a well marked page. Jo stopped to read it and plopped back on the couch. Well, she had wanted a definition, and here it was.

Love is patient and kind; Love does not envy nor
Boast, it is not arrogant or
Rude. It does not insist on it's own way;
It is not irritable or resentful; It does
Not rejoice at wrongdoing, but
Rejoices with the Truth. Love bears all
Things, believes all things, hopes all things, endures
All things. Love never
Ends. ~ 1 Corinthians 13:4-8

Jo sat in stunned silence a while, thinking over
what she had just read. Okay, that was just a little
too complicated to just be a coincidence.

The passage kept going through her mind as she
worked the rest of the day.

She was still a little preoccupied when she was
lighting the oven to bake some rolls for dinner and
somehow managed to catch part of her hair on fire.
She got it out by pulling the towel she was using to
handle the pans over her head However, now she
looked half scalped, so grabbed the scissors and
finished the job.

When Will came back over, later, he stared at her
in shock.

"What happened?"

"Oh, just a little fire."

"Jo, are you okay? Did you get hurt at all?"

"No, just my feelings for being so careless." She
was feeling a little sheepish for not paying attention
while handling fire.

"It's only hair, if you want, it will grow back, but you are what is important."

Will was just happy that she was unhurt. He had to make sure she really was unhurt and hugged her to him, rocking back and forth.

"I'm just so glad you are okay."

Jo was surprised. She always thought her hair was her only feature that the guys liked. She actually thought Will would turn away from her now that she had chopped off hair. This made her think that he was telling her his true feelings, when he said he loved her.

She relaxed into his arms and it felt so right to be there. Slowly, they looked at each other, and gently, he kissed her. Then he loosened his arms and stepped back.

She was a little flustered, but felt happy inside, too. They could work out any differences they had and plan what they wanted from each other and life. For now, they would keep learning more about each other and get better acquainted. With all they had planned, they would have plenty of chances, working together. The cabin addition, the research he was doing and the book they were planning, together.

Epilogue

It was a lovely autumn day. Jo's parents finally were here, at the cabin and amazed at how lovely everything was.

The spare room had been built onto the back of the cabin and turned into two extra rooms by the time they were done with it. A larger bunkhouse sat beside the original little bunkhouse, so there was room for guests.

Will's Mom had came up, also. After all, it isn't every day an only son gets married. At least she hoped not.

All of their friends, locally, from Fairbanks and from the village were gathered. Most of the bugs were absent, though.

Jo nervously adjusted her bridal outfit, thinking maybe she should have stuck with the canvas pants and T-shirt. Her mother pushed her hands down and told her she looked beautiful.

Lorraine and Sue were ready to march down the aisle between the benches Will and Jo had made just for the wedding. The aisle was a cleared strip of gravel between the benches leading to a little floored area they could use for dancing, after the wedding. The Pastor from the village waited under the golden trees shading the area. Sun shown down through the trees and shared it's warmth on this golden day.

Her dad stood waiting in the doorway of the cabin. He certainly had never expected to not only come to Alaska, but to come to his oldest daughter's wedding in Alaska. He could tell she loved it here and her choice of husband could not be faulted. He felt rather guilty for having pushed her at Bill Humphries. He just had wanted to keep her close to home.

The little band that sometimes played at the roadhouse started up on their own version of the Wedding March and it was time to start.

Jo's Mom went to her seat with Thad and Harlan escorting her. Lorraine and Sue started down the aisle. Jo's Dad held out his arm and asked if she were ready. Yes, yes she was ready. This was the start of a whole new chapter in her life. The one that started right where 'Happily Ever After' left off..

www.ingramcontent.com/pod-product-compliance
Lightning Source LLC
Chambersburg PA
CBHW070922260626
47162CB00007B/2764